SPECIAL
ASSIGNMENT

Other books by Kathleen Fuller:

Santa Fe Sunrise

SPECIAL ASSIGNMENT

•

Kathleen Fuller

AVALON BOOKS
NEW YORK

PRINTED IN THE UNITED STATES OF AMERICA
ON ACID-FREE PAPER
BY HADDON CRAFTSMEN, BLOOMSBURG, PENNSYLVANIA

To Jim and Karmen Daly,
and Steve and Pat Bosch.

Blood is thicker than water.
I love you guys.

A special thank you to Eric Spangler from
Family Life Ministries, and Danita Harris,
morning news anchor for WEWS in
Cleveland, Ohio, for their willingness
to share their knowledge and experiences
in broadcast journalism.

Chapter One

Late! Eve Norwood silently cursed herself for wearing three-inch heels as she hurried down the hallway. How could she have overslept? During her four years as a news reporter for WCBH she'd never arrived late—not to the station, not to an assignment. She prided herself on three things—professionalism, presentation, and punctuality.

This morning she was striking out on all three.

Juggling her purse and briefcase, she scrambled past the receptionist. "Have they started yet, Rebecca?" Eve called out on her way to the conference room.

"Five minutes ago!"

Eve picked up the pace, nearly skidding by the doorway of the room. She took a deep, calming

1

breath, slung her purse over her shoulder, and smoothed her skirt. Tucking a thick strand of hair behind her ear, she groaned when she felt her naked earlobe. No time to search her purse for a pair of earrings. Brushing the hair back over her ear, she opened the door and casually walked into the room, as if being late for the meeting had been her intent all along.

Seven pairs of eyes, including her new boss', were aimed directly at her. Her cheeks grew warm, but she didn't offer an excuse. Instead, she slipped into the first empty chair she saw, ignored the questioning glances, and dug through her handbag for a pad and pencil.

Jason Brook, the station's investigative reporter, made a big production of checking his wristwatch. "Never thought I'd see the day Eve Norwood would be late for anything," he said in a loud whisper to no one in particular. "Especially work."

Eve looked up to see him eyeing her squarely.

"You must have had a hot date this weekend," he added with a touch of smarminess.

She gave him a cool smile, but revealed nothing. When he flashed the grin that got him more female viewer mail than any other station employee, she knew he was flirting with her. Again.

It was no secret at the station that he'd been trying to go out with her for months. When would he get the picture—she didn't date men she worked with. She'd done that once before. Never would she be naive enough to get involved with a co-worker again.

Brianne Lagan, WCBH's recently hired news director, tapped her pencil against the table. "If you're done with the chitchat, Brook, I'd like to get back to business."

Eve watched with satisfaction as the smile slid from Jason's face.

She listened carefully as Brianne gave the reporters their assignments for the day. The petite, energetic woman had been at the station for only a few weeks, but her take-charge attitude and total commitment to her job had garnered Eve's respect. News directors often changed jobs faster than you could learn to spell their last names. But Eve hoped Brianne would stick around. She seemed genuine, if a little over-driven.

Thirty minutes later, Brianne slipped her tortoise shell reading glasses off her nose. "That's it, people. Now get out there and bring us back those stories. Let's show Youngsville who's number one in news." Repeating the station's tagline would have sounded ridiculous coming from anyone else, but the intensity behind the news director's words had everyone nodding their heads enthusiastically as they left the room.

Everyone except Eve.

She slowly rose from the table, stunned. Where

was her assignment? She'd always been given one, even if it was something as mundane as covering garden club meetings. Lately she'd been getting juicier stories, giving her more on-air time and exposure. Was ignoring her Brianne's way of reprimanding her for being late?

But Brianne walked toward her. "Eve. I'd like to talk to you."

"Sure," Eve replied, a little wary. "Again, I'm sorry I was late—"

Brianne waved her hand. "Don't worry about it. Everyone's late once in a while. Just don't make it a habit."

"I won't."

"You're probably wondering why I didn't give you an assignment," the news director continued. She motioned for Eve to sit down again, and lowered herself into the next chair. "I have something different in mind for you. Graham mentioned before he left that you had approached him with an idea for a feature series."

Eve searched her mind, trying to think of what Brianne was referring to. She couldn't recall discussing anything with Graham Billington, the former news director. He hadn't exactly been open to new ideas.

"I know Graham didn't think much of it, but I believe it's a great suggestion. Sure, hard news sells, but our viewers need to know about the positive things happening in our community."

Understanding began to dawn. "The 'Everyday Heroes' feature," Eve said, nodding her head.

"Exactly." Brianne pushed a stray auburn curl back from her forehead. "We're thinking about making it a weekly series. You would do reports about individuals and businesses that are doing things to improve Youngsville and the surrounding area. We'll air it on the six P.M. newscast. What do you think?"

Eve felt her excitement building. Her own series, aired during the highest rated time slot on the schedule. Her mind whirled as she thought of the exposure she'd get, of the reports she could add to her audition tape that Elizabeth, her agent, was currently circulating around New York. This might be the assignment that would lead to her big break into one of the national networks.

Her lips curved into the smile she reserved for the camera. "You can count on me, Brianne," Eve assured her. "Doing this series will be no problem."

"Well, whether it becomes a series is up to you," she said. "Are you familiar with Brewster Farm?"

Eve nodded. "Every August they put on a four-day summer festival. All the proceeds go to the Foreman Cancer Center."

"Today's the first day of the festival, and I want you to cover it. The cameraman will edit the report on site and upload it for tonight's six o'clock broadcast. Depending on viewer response, we'll take a look at making it into a series. I'm assuming you have some ideas for future stories."

"Absolutely." Eve reached for her purse and stood, ready for the challenge. She'd make sure her series became a reality. "Will Jackie be coming with me?" she asked, referring to the camerawoman who usually filmed her reports.

"No, I've hired a freelancer for this job. All our regular people are booked up with other assignments." Brianne rose and walked back to the head of the table. "It's an unbelievable stroke of luck that we got him. He used to work for NBC, was one of their international cameramen. Even won an Emmy for his work in the Middle East."

Eve's stomach lurched as her boss continued talking. *It couldn't be . . . surely it's a coincidence . . . there must be several cameramen working for NBC in the Middle East . . .*

Brianne picked up a stack of papers and tapped the bottom of it against the table. "You might know him, he used to work here." She looked at Eve. "Does the name Toby Myers ring a bell?"

Eve's hand clutched the back of the chair. The name Toby Myers did more than ring a bell—it sounded off dozens of warning sirens in her head.

Toby Myers shoved his hands into the pockets of his worn jeans and leaned back against the side of the WCBH news van. He tried for a casual pose, but inside his nerves were shredded. For the hundredth time he asked himself why he was here, why he left a high-profile job at a national network to return to his hometown of Youngsville, and to this particular station.

But he knew the reason why. He needed something familiar. Something grounding. Still, he found himself pondering the irony that the one station willing to hire him was his former employer, and his first assignment just happened to be with his former girlfriend.

He tapped his brown suede hiking boot against the parking lot's black asphalt, the heat emanating from the ground. The bright morning sun caused perspiration to break out on the back of his neck. Where was she? Was she doing this to him on purpose, making him wait because of what happened between them in the past? He hated waiting, and she knew it.

Not that he could blame her for being mad at him. He'd be the first to admit he'd screwed up. Royally. *Who leaves town without saying good-*

*bye? Especially right after your girlfriend tells
you she loves you? A jerk, that's who.*

Yet a part of him was eager to see her again. To
smooth things over with her. Maybe they would
even become friends.

Toby checked his watch: 10:30. Eve was supposed to meet him at the van at a quarter after. He
was impatient to get started, looking forward to
working on an assignment that didn't involve acts
of war. His stint as a cameraman in the Middle
East had exposed him to enough of that.

The clicking sound of heels against pavement
caused him to turn his head. Through the dark
shields of his sunglasses he saw a woman heading
toward him, her chin-length hair fluttering around
her cheeks as she walked. She appeared to have
the same medium height and slim build as Eve
Norwood, but he still couldn't make out her features, which were partially covered by a nice pair
of black-tinted glasses.

As she neared he could tell it was Eve all right.
But the casual pants and shirt she'd favored as an
intern were gone, replaced by a crisp, dark blue
business suit. And when did she become a blond?

He shifted on his feet as she approached. With
deliberate steps she walked up to him and extended her hand. "Toby," she said in a voice steady and
resonant from years of on-camera reporting. "It's
been a long time."

Pulling his hand out of his pocket, he reached for hers and shook it, amazed at the softness of her palm. Had her hands always been this soft? Surely he would have remembered that. Wouldn't he?

Realizing he had been holding her hand longer than necessary, he hastily let go of it. "Good to see you, Eve," he said, feeling the need to fill the awkward silence between them.

He saw her chin lift slightly. "Wish I could say the same."

"Eve, I—"

"We have an assignment to do," she said, moving toward the passenger side of the van. "Are you ready to go?"

So that's how she's going to play it. "Sure," he said, yanking open his door and fishing the van keys out of his pocket. He slid into his seat, started the engine, and eased it out of the parking deck and onto Main Street. He reached for the air conditioning controls and flipped them to high.

"Brewster Farm," she said, her hand shooting out and adjusting the air conditioner level to low.

"What?"

"Our assignment. Brewster Farm. You do know where that is, don't you?"

"Of course. I grew up here, the same as you."

"I thought you might have forgotten the directions."

He cast a sideways glance, not missing the cutting edge in her voice. "I haven't been gone that long." He raised the air conditioner temperature up another notch. "Do you mind?" he asked, welcoming the blast of almost-cool air. "It's sweltering in here."

"Yes I do mind," she replied, turning the knob back down. "It's blowing on my hair."

For crying out loud. He hadn't expected her to make this easy. But her coldness seemed so out of character from the Eve Norwood he remembered. *So much for being friends. She's making me sweat in more ways than one.*

After turning off Main and catching the freeway, they'd gone several miles in uncomfortable silence while Toby searched for something to say. "How's your mom?" he asked, grasping for a suitable topic of conversation. Anything to end the oppressive silence that filled the van. He'd met Pauline Norwood only one time, but he'd liked her immediately. He'd also been well aware of how close Eve was to her mother.

"She died last year. Cancer."

Toby wanted to smack himself upside the head for being so insensitive. "I'm sorry," he said, knowing the words were inadequate.

"Thanks," she said curtly. After a few moments she asked, "How about your parents?"

"They're still in California. Usually they spend summers in San Jose with my sister Hannah, and the winters in Florida. They should be back there by the middle of September."

More silence. This time Toby decided to let it ride, not wanting to put his foot in his mouth any more than he already had.

Moments later Eve picked up her purse and began digging in it like a dog searching for a treasured bone. She seemed to grow more agitated by the second as her exploration proved fruitless.

"What are you looking for?"

"None of your business," she snapped, her hands still foraging.

"C'mon Eve, don't be this way."

She looked up from the purse, and he could feel her gaze flinging daggers into his profile. "What way? Insensitive? Inconsiderate? Oh, pardon me, I forgot. Those are *your* personality traits."

Keeping his eyes on the road, Toby's hands twisted back and forth on the steering wheel. "Look," he began, keeping his focus on the road, "it wasn't my idea for us to work together. But now that we are, we should try to make the best of it." Out of the corner of his eye he saw her head drop against the back of the seat.

"I know," she said quietly, her formerly venomous tone gone. "This doesn't have anything to do with us. You and I working together is simply a coincidence."

He set the van on cruise control and risked

another quick look at her. "Eve, what I wanted to tell you earlier . . . well, I want you to know I'm sorry for what happened between us."

"Are you talking about our relationship? Or about the way you dumped me?"

Her tone was drenched in sarcasm, but he could detect the note of hurt in it. Before he could reply, he heard her sigh.

"Never mind," she said. "It was a long time ago. I was young—and stupid. I should have known better than to get involved with someone I worked with."

"You weren't stupid—"

"Really, Toby, none of it matters anymore," she said, cutting him off. "What happened between us is in the past. I want to keep it there. We're both adults, professionals. I'm sure we can work together on this assignment without letting any personal feelings get in the way."

"Sure . . . professionals." He was surprised at the sudden change in her composure. Minutes ago she'd lashed out at him, now she was talking as if they'd never shared anything more intimate than a pencil. Apparently, the feelings she'd had for him four years ago were now completely gone.

It left him surprisingly disappointed.

Chapter Two

Halfway to the Brewsters, Eve retrieved her cell phone from her purse. Toby listened while she deftly punched the numbers on the keypad. After a few minutes of more dialing and listening, he surmised she was checking her messages. From the small groan she let out before turning off the phone, she obviously didn't like what she heard.

Picking up her purse a second time, she dropped the phone inside and once again resumed her earlier search. "Aha!" She triumphantly jerked her hand out of the bag.

"Found what you were looking for?"

"Yes. I knew I had a pair in here somewhere."

Toby caught sight of her inserting something

shiny and gold into her earlobe. "You went through all that trouble for a pair of earrings?"

"It was worth it." She flipped her head to the side and put on the other earring. "I finally feel completely dressed."

"You looked pretty good before." The words were out of his mouth before he could stop them. *Where had that come from?* His face heated up, and he was thankful he'd kept the full beard he'd grown while working in Tel Aviv. The last thing he wanted was Eve seeing him blushing like an awkward teenager.

Quickly he changed the subject. "So, have you been to the Summer Festival before?"

She didn't answer right away, as if she didn't want to be drawn into a conversation with him. "No," she finally replied, reverting to her earlier coolness.

"From what Brianne told me it sounds great. Seems like I missed out on something fun while I was away."

Eve let out a curt laugh. "I can't see you at a farm, Toby."

"Why not?"

"Well, you have to admit a hoedown isn't exactly your style. For one thing, they don't play the rock music loud enough. Remember the time we went to that club, the music was so loud—" Abruptly she stopped.

"We couldn't hear each other," he said, completing the thought for her. "And the smoke was too thick."

A pause. "You didn't seem to mind," she murmured.

"I didn't."

Suddenly she clamped her hand on his arm. "Toby, slow down! You're going to miss the exit!" Releasing her grip, she pointed at a green sign on the side of the freeway. "Make a right at the end of the ramp. The farm is about a mile down the road."

Leaning over, she snatched her purse from the floorboard again and fished inside the seemingly bottomless black leather bag. Pulling out a bright green compact, she whisked off her sunglasses.

Seconds later Brewster Farm came into view. The festival was in full swing by the time they pulled into the cordoned-off grass area serving as a parking lot. Toby cut the engine while Eve applied a coat of red lipstick to her lips. Seeing her primp was something he was used to. Nearly all the female reporters he'd worked with were obsessive about their looks.

When he exited the van, the rich aroma of freshly mowed hay surrounded him in the strong heat of the midmorning. Eve met him at the driver's side door. "Where do you think we should start first?"

Turning at the sound of her voice, her question

immediately flew out of his mind. As he took his first good look at her without her sunglasses, his heartbeat instantly shot out of rhythm. Her straight blond hair shone like silk, the gold-colored strands reflecting the bright rays in the warm summer sunlight. She looked good as a blond. *Real good.* A gentle late August breeze carried the faint scent of her perfume to him, over-riding the earthy aroma of the farm with a flowery feminine smell he found extremely appealing.

Who was he kidding? He found *all* of her extremely appealing. The intense attraction he felt for her at that moment was more frightening—and more exhilarating—than he'd ever experienced before.

This wasn't what he expected at all.

He's not what I expected.

Ten minutes after they arrived at Brewster, Toby started giving Eve instructions, but she suddenly couldn't focus on what he was saying. Looking up at him, butterflies began to flit in her stomach and her palms grew damp and slick. It had been more than a year since she'd been nervous in front of the camera. She'd thought she'd had her feelings under control when she first saw him.

Why was she letting him get to her like this now?

You looked pretty good to me. His words floated unbidden through her head. It had taken everything she had to pretend she hadn't heard his compliment. But the words had touched her, the thought of them still affecting her now. *How infuriating.*

Outwardly, she could see Toby Myers hadn't changed much since the last time she'd seen him. He stood several inches taller than her five-foot-six frame, enough that she had to tilt her head back to look him straight in the eye. His black, unruly hair curled around his ears and at the back of his neck, covering the collar of his shirt. It was a little longer than the current fashion, but the length suited him. He still seemed to favor casual dress—a white polo shirt and faded blue jeans that fit his muscular build all too well. The only thing different about his appearance was the neatly trimmed beard that covered his square jaw. She'd always disliked beards.

What does it matter if I like his beard or not? I'm not supposed to like him at all.

But there was something different about him, something she couldn't put her finger on. His arrogant swagger was gone. His apology in the van had thrown her off balance. She couldn't recall him ever saying he was sorry for anything during their relationship. Even when he'd been late picking her up for dates he hadn't uttered a word of apology, instead acting as if she should feel privileged he'd showed up at all. Yet the apology he offered an hour ago had seemed genuinely sincere, making her emotions more unsettled.

She didn't want him to be different. She wanted to remember him the way he was. A conceited jerk. A self-absorbed jerk. A jerk who had held her heart in his hands, then threw it away as if it was worthless trash.

"Eve? Are you listening to me?" His voice pierced her thoughts.

She snapped back to attention, resolving to keep her focus on her job and not on her past with Toby Myers. "Of course I am."

"Then what did I just say?"

"You said . . ." The dampness of her palms increased as she tried to remember what he'd told her. He'd taken off his sunglasses, and the way he was staring at her with those intoxicating chocolate-colored eyes made concentrating difficult. She couldn't deny that he was an extraordinarily handsome man. He always had been.

"You said . . . um, you thought it would be a good idea to interview the Brewsters first." She had no idea if he'd said that or not, but it seemed logical.

He lifted one dark brown brow. "Not exactly, but that's close enough." He placed his hands on his slim hips and scanned the crowds milling in the area. "I wonder where they are?"

Eve followed his gaze. All around them groups of children and adults could be seen enjoying the warm cloudless day. To the far left of the field stood a huge corn maze, and the joyous laughter of several youngsters filling the air as they passed through the tall green stalks. Although fall was still a couple of weeks away, an impressive patch of orange pumpkins was grouped a few feet from a large, sun-weathered barn. On the right Eve noticed a large horseshoe pit fenced in with chicken wire. The clanging sound of heavy horseshoes hitting against metal stakes mingled with the excited shouts and exasperated groans of the players. Brewster Farm was a very nice place.

"See if you can locate the Brewsters," Toby said, drawing her out of her musings. He searched the landscape again. "We'll do the interview . . . there." He pointed to the corn field, the tips of the stalks swaying slightly in the breeze. "By the maze will work. The light's good, and the corn will make a great backdrop. Meanwhile I'll take a look around and see where we can do a couple of standups. Then I'll get my equipment and meet you and the Brewsters in twenty minutes or so."

"Anything else?" she asked, glowering at him. Although she was used to cameramen calling the shots on location, it galled her to take orders from *him*. Old resentment rose again, resentment she'd thought she'd buried years ago. "Shall I fetch your camera for you too? Why don't I peel you a grape while I'm at it?"

"Don't be ridiculous, Eve," he said, his countenance darkening. "I can get my equipment myself."

"Are you sure? I wouldn't want to be accused of being a slacker."

He furrowed his brows. "I thought we declared a truce."

She folded her arms across her chest. "I didn't know we were at war."

"You could have fooled me."

Dropping her arms, she whirled around and turned her back on him. "Let's just get through the assignment, okay?" she called out over her shoulder.

"Agreed. Oh, and Eve?"

She stopped and turned to face him. "What now?"

"I don't like grapes." The corners of his mouth twitched slightly. "But you can peel me a banana anytime."

"Oooh . . ." Spinning around without answering, Eve seethed as she crossed the field in search of the Brewsters. She ignored the curious glances of the festival attendees who happened to recognize her from the evening news.

Her rational mind knew she'd been unreasonable in lashing out at him. He was merely doing his job. Any good cameraman would have given her the same directions.

She wasn't sure who she was angrier with—

Toby, for turning on the charm she'd always found hard to resist, or with herself for wanting to smile at his lame comment in spite of her irritation with him. His ability to defuse a tense situation by cracking a joke or flashing a smile had always been something she appreciated about him.

Right now she found it annoying.

Her dark blue pump sank into a brown, smelly pile left behind by one of the Brewsters' animals. She groaned as she removed her expensive shoe, then scraped the side and bottom of it on a patch of clean grass. There were traces of hay and brown gunk that wouldn't come off. "That's just great. I'm going to reek of cow manure."

Slipping her shoe back on, she continued walking. "Better get it together," she mumbled. "I can't let him get to me like this. I won't let him ruin what I've worked so hard for."

Chapter Three

Less than twenty minutes later, Eve found the Brewsters organizing an apple bobbing contest in the barn. Mrs. Brewster, or Gladys, as she insisted on being called, was thrilled her "little festival" was getting news coverage. She talked nonstop as she and her taciturn husband left the contest and walked across the field with Eve to meet Toby.

"I watch Newschannel Seven every evening," the portly woman gushed. "It's my favorite newscast. I think that young man Jason Brook is such a wonderful reporter."

Figures. What female between 10 and 90 didn't think he was a great reporter?

"You're good too, Ms. Norwood," she added. "I

especially liked that story you did on price fixing at the grocery store. Because of you, I started doing my shopping at Brinkman's Food Stop. They're a little more expensive, but at least they treat their customers fair." She paused in her monologue, her hand shaking slightly as she smoothed back a few strands of gray hair that had escaped the bun at the back of her neck. "Do I look okay? I've never been on TV before. I'm a little nervous." Tugging at her light blue denim skirt, she gave Eve a worried glance.

Eve smiled. "You look fine, Gladys. There's nothing to be nervous about. It's not as hard as you think. I'll ask you a few easy questions about the festival, and you tell me everything about this wonderful event. Just ignore the camera, and relax. You'll be great."

"Okay, if you're sure . . ."

"I'm sure," Eve responded sincerely. "I know you'll be a natural at this."

They arrived at the maze to find Toby ready, his ENG camera balanced on his shoulder. On his *broad* shoulder, Eve noticed, giving her head a hard shake. *Focus, focus.*

"Toby Myers," he introduced himself, extending his free hand first to George, then to Gladys. "Why don't you two stand over there? Ms. Norwood will join you shortly."

The Brewsters moved into position by one of the rows while Eve retrieved her microphone. "Ready to do this?" he asked.

She unwound the microphone cord. "Let's just get it over with."

"Eve," he said, moving closer to her. His voice was low in her ear. "It doesn't have to be like this between us. We're on the same side, you know." Stepping back, he called out to the Brewsters. "Okay, we're all set."

As she walked the few steps toward the couple, Eve's stomach knotted up as if this was her first interview. What had she told Gladys only moments ago? To relax? Why couldn't she follow her own advice? Closing her eyes, she forced Toby out of her mind.

It took only seconds for Eve to regain her composure, and the interview was underway. Soon she was able to ignore the camera and the man behind it, becoming completely engrossed in her work. Taking care to set the Brewsters at ease, she asked them simple, open-ended questions about their farm and the activities. Her admiration for the couple quickly grew as they explained why they decided to start the Summer Festival.

"Our only daughter, Janet, died of leukemia ten years ago," Gladys said. "She wasn't expected to live longer than thirty-five years, but the good Lord saw fit to leave her with us for five more. Toward the end of her illness we got to know the folks at the cancer center pretty well. I began volunteering there a couple of years after Janet died. It seems there's always a need for research money." She spread her arms, gesturing to the wide expanse of farmland. George stood next to her, nodding his agreement. "It didn't take us long to figure out that our farm would be a great place to have a fundraiser, and the idea kind of blossomed from there."

Gladys' eyes grew moist. George wrapped his arm around her and she leaned against him. "It does us good to have all the children here, enjoying this. Janet was our only one, you see, and of course she couldn't have any children. So having all the young ones here every summer is a blessing to us."

Eve found it difficult to speak past the lump that had suddenly formed in her throat. The sting of tears filled her eyes, but she blinked them back. Gladys' words opened a wound deep inside Eve, bringing painful memories to the surface. How could this couple talk about blessings when their only child had died?

After the interview ended, Toby came up behind Eve. "Great job, Gladys," he said, removing the camera from his shoulder.

"Is that all you need from us?" George asked in a gruff voice, speaking for the first time.

Toby nodded. "Yes, but I'd like to get some footage of the festival before we leave."

"Sure." Gladys wiped her cheeks with her fingers. "Stay as long as you want. Film away," she added with a smile. Reaching for Eve's hand, she gave it a squeeze. "When you're done, maybe you two can stay and enjoy yourselves for a little while. The hayrides last all afternoon."

Was it her imagination, or did Eve see a mischievous twinkle in the older woman's eye? "No, we couldn't possibly," she blurted out a bit too quickly, the thought of she and Toby being in such close proximity dredging up memories better left alone.

Toby tossed Eve a strange look before returning his attention to Gladys. "Thank you for the generous offer, but Eve's right. We have to get back to the station as soon as we're through here."

"I understand," Gladys replied kindly. "You two have a safe trip back to town, but if you change your mind . . ." She let her voice trail off as she gave them a knowing smile before turning and following her husband back to the barn.

Toby looked at Eve as the Brewsters faded in the distance. "Tempted?" he teased, the hint of a smile playing on his lips.

A torrent of emotions surged through her as she remained under his scrutiny. For a moment the years of separation and hurt between them melted. She was drawn toward him, despite every fiber of her being fighting against it. She didn't want to be this close, not when she could easily drown in the depths of his eyes, the teasing spark in them suddenly fading into a dusky intensity.

Moving away, she hastily averted her gaze and busied herself with winding up the microphone cord. "You said you wanted to get more footage," she mumbled, pretending to be intent on her task.

He cleared his throat and hoisted his camera back on his shoulder. "Right." He paused. "You have to admit, they are an amazing couple," he said, watching the Brewsters as they disappeared inside the barn. "The courage they have to open their home and their property to strangers . . . to children." He shook his head. "Simply amazing."

Eve didn't reply. Sure, they were amazing. They were also fools for being surrounded by reminders of something they could never have.

"I wanted to get shots of the different activities going on here," Toby continued. "I also think you should do another standup, probably by that huge sign near the front entrance. We'll film that last."

"Fine," she said, relieved they were getting back to business. The job at hand was neutral ground. As long as her attention stayed on her work, she could handle being around him. She would simply have to make sure nothing personal came between them.

It was the only way she could survive the rest of the assignment.

* * *

After the interview Toby spent another hour filming, then began the editing process using the AV equipment in the back of the station's van. During that time Eve recorded some voice–overs for the piece, then sat in the front seat and checked her answering machine twice. Her disappointment at not hearing from her agent made her want to throw the cell phone out the window.

Since she first began working in television news, her ultimate goal had been to land a job at a national network. Everything she'd done during the course of her career had been geared to making that happen. But after three years of her agent making the rounds with Eve's audition tape, none of the New York stations showed any interest.

Elizabeth encouraged her to be patient, telling her that she was still young and had time to build up her reputation. But at 27, Eve didn't feel all that young. Every year the station hired a new crop of reporters fresh from internships, hungry to add to their own audition reels. Few were content to remain at a middle market station for very long.

It made Toby's decision to leave NBC and move back to Youngsville even more mystifying. Why the step backward? Why give up what many people worked years to achieve?

"Eve?" she heard him call from the back. "Come take a look and see if this will work."

Moments later she was sitting next to him in

the small confines of the van, surrounded by electronic editing equipment. "I can see why Brianne says you're one of her best reporters," he said, queuing up the segment. "You did a great job."

A small measure of warmth ran through her. That Brianne thought she was good stroked her professional ego, but the words ran deeper because Toby had said them. As much as she wanted to, she couldn't deny that his opinion of her work meant something to her. It always had.

She watched as the finished segment flashed on the small monitor, amazed at how well he'd put the piece together in such a short period of time. Grudgingly, she had to admit that he'd made her look good.

"I wish I'd had a couple of more hours to play around with it," he said. "But this will have to do. The station wanted the upload in by five." He checked his watch. "Ten minutes 'til. Any last-minute changes you want me to make?"

"No." A smile spread across her face, knowing Brianne would be pleased. Eve knew the weekly assignment would be hers.

"Glad you like it. Give me a few minutes to send it through, and we can head back." Grinning, he pressed a large red button. "That wasn't so bad, was it?"

She swallowed. Forget Jason Brook and his

thousand-watt smile. He had nothing on Toby. "I guess not."

"I think we make a pretty good team." He retrieved the laptop computer on his right. "Professionally speaking, of course." He halted his movements and sniffed the air, then looked at her. "Did you step in something out there?"

"Great. Just great!" Bursting out of the van she stomped to an open area a few steps away. Yanking off her shoe, she ground the bottom of it against the flattened grass of the makeshift parking lot. Hearing a low chuckle, she spun around and caught him making a halfhearted attempt to contain his laughter.

"It's not funny!" She held up the offending pump. "These are very expensive shoes!"

"Sorry." He forced a straight face. "I'm sure they are. I promise I won't mention it again."

"You better not," she warned, shaking the shoe at him. "Or you'll find this upside your head."

At that point he lost it, breaking into hearty laughter. "I can just see us explaining to the boss why we both smell like the back end of a horse!"

Suddenly it struck her how ridiculous she looked, standing there raising her smelly shoe like a deadly weapon. She began to laugh, the day's tension draining away as she continued to giggle.

After wrapping her offending shoe in a few layers of old newspaper and placing it in the back corner of the van, they pulled out of the Brewsters' parking lot and headed back to the station. Eve slipped her other shoe off, and didn't say a word when Toby turned up the air conditioner.

"Hungry?" he asked, sounding more relaxed than he had all day. "Since we skipped lunch, I thought we could stop at that fast food place I saw near the freeway exit."

She frowned. The ice may have broken between them, but she wasn't in a hurry to test the water. "I really need to get back to the station."

"You've got to eat, Eve. And even if you don't think you have to, I'm starving."

Her stomach rumbled. Placing her palm on her flat belly to muffle the sound, she agreed. "Okay." *What could one hamburger hurt?*

"Great!" he said, activating the turn signal as the golden arches came into view.

"The drive-through," she ordered as he turned into the parking lot.

He maneuvered the van behind a long row of waiting cars, then set the brake and turned to her. "No problem." His lips curled into another devastating smile.

Her thrumming heartbeat echoed loudly in her ears as their gazes locked. *Oh Toby, you're wrong . . . so wrong. This is going to be a huge problem.*

Chapter Four

Toby finished the last bite of his triple cheese-burger as he steered the WCBH news van down the freeway. Reaching for the super-size soft drink sitting in the cup holder, he glanced at Eve as she nibbled on a golden French fry. While he had practically shoved his entire hamburger in his mouth in an attempt to appease his growling stomach, most of her chicken sandwich and fries lay neatly spread on a double layer of napkins on her lap. She possessed a poise and grace he hadn't been aware of before now.

"You've changed," he suddenly said.

Eve swallowed. "Pardon me?"

"You know . . . over the years . . . uh, people change." *Great, now I sound like a babbling idiot.*

"Are you talking about my hair?"

Confused, he glanced at her again. "Your hair?"

"I know it was brown when you left. But actually I was born a blond. It kept getting darker over time, so I decided to go back to my natural color."

"Well . . . I wasn't exactly talking about your hair," he said, barely following her thread of conversation. "But it's . . ."

"It's what?" she asked, a warning edge to her voice.

"Nice," he said, wondering how he'd gotten off track so quickly. Discussing Eve's hair color wasn't what he wanted to talk about at all.

"Thanks," she said, then took a sip of her drink.

The skyline of the city of Youngsville was now in view, and although he'd pretty much made a fool of himself already, he continued to press on with the conversation. "I'd like to think I've changed too."

She dabbed at her lips with a spare napkin. "Really?" Her response was chilly. "I hadn't noticed." She picked up another fry.

He pulled the van into the lot, found a space, then put the vehicle in park. "C'mon Eve, I'm trying to make amends here. Can't you at least cut me a little slack?"

She remained quiet.

"I know leaving the way I did was wrong," he continued.

"You finally got something right."

He ignored her barb. "But like you said, that was a long time ago, and things are different. *I'm* different."

"You're assuming I actually care." Her tone dripped with contempt. Snatching her purse from the floorboard, she gave him a steely glare. "At one time I might have felt . . . something for you." Her voice faltered slightly. "But you destroyed it, so pardon me for my lack of interest in your life."

Toby shut his eyes briefly against the pain he heard in her words. Pain she was trying gallantly to hide, but was there nevertheless. Pain he had caused. The guilt was nearly overwhelming. "Eve," he said, opening his eyes. "What can I do to make it up to you?"

Her eyes hardened into chips of blue ice. "Nothing. There's nothing I want from you, Toby. You made your feelings on our relationship perfectly clear when you left me." She bolted out of the van and slammed the door.

Scrambling out of his seatbelt, he flung open his own door and ran to the back of the van, only to see her fleeing in stockinged feet to the building entrance. "Eve!" he called out, but the heavy metal door banged shut behind her as her name escaped his lips.

He turned and pounded his fist against the side

of the still-running van, oblivious to the jolt of pain that shot up his arm. *Way to go, genius.*

Her eyes burning, Eve sprinted across the lobby toward the elevator. Swallowing hard, she forced the moisture away, refusing to let Toby reduce her to tears. Hadn't she cried oceans of them over him in the past?

Mashing the "up" button several times, she paced in front of the mirrored elevator doors. Feeling the cold tile floor through her hose, she glanced down at her feet and sighed. She might look ridiculous standing there without her shoes, but no way was she going back to face Toby again. Not in a million years. They could keep stinking up the van for all she cared.

She stopped pacing, and leaned back against the wall, trying to rein in her emotions. But it was difficult, since at that moment she hated Toby Myers with a red-hot passion. Without a doubt he brought out the worst in her. Which was sadly ironic.

Because at one time he had brought out the best.

Back at her cubicle, Eve retrieved the pair of plain white sneakers and white socks she kept in the bottom drawer of her desk. Her silky hose were full of holes and runs from the asphalt parking lot. Scowling, she put on the socks and shoes, then left her cubicle to seek out Brianne.

She found the station manager in her office, poring over reams of paperwork. A half-eaten turkey sandwich on a Stryofoam plate sat at her left, a mug of steaming coffee was at her right.

"Gearing up for a long night?"

"As always." With her hand, Brianne motioned for Eve to enter. Slipping off her reading glasses, she gestured to the small chair across from her desk. "Great work on the Brewster piece, Eve. Wonderful story. We've already received e-mails from several viewers, all positive. Some even wanted to know where they could send a donation to the cancer center." She smiled. "Congratulations. Looks like you and Toby have that series after all."

Eve threaded her fingers together and pressed her hands into her lap. "That's what I wanted to talk to you about."

Brianne's smile faded. "Is there a problem?"

"Yes. I mean, no. Well, nothing that can't be fixed." She took a deep breath. "I want to request another cameraman."

"Out of the question."

Eve's fingers tightened their grip. "Why not? We have several cameramen here who could do as good a job." Silently she conceded none of them were better than Toby.

"Yes, we do have good cameramen here. But I don't understand why you can't work with Toby.

He's one of the best cameramen I've ever seen. I would have thought you'd be grateful for the opportunity."

Grateful? She felt anything but grateful. "Suffice it to say we have our differences," she hedged. "Differences I believe might affect our working relationship."

Brianne looked at her for a long moment. "You'll have to learn to get over them," she said, putting down her pen. "I'm not taking him off this assignment. He agreed to work here as a free-lancer only, and I can't risk the chance of him going to another station because you don't get along with him. Whatever issues you have with Toby, solve them. I don't care how, but make sure it doesn't affect the work." She reached for her coffee mug, peering over the rim before taking a sip. "Or should I be looking for another reporter to do the series?"

"No." Thin fingers of panic gripped her at the idea of losing a major assignment. "That won't be necessary."

"Good." Brianne picked up her reading glasses and regarded Eve thoughtfully. "A word of advice," she said, the harsh lines around her brown eyes softening. "Don't mix business and pleasure. It never works. Trust me, I know." A glimmer of regret passed over her face before she blanked her features.

Eve wondered if the warning stemmed from personal experience.

Brianne put her reading glasses back on and scanned the paperwork on her desk. "Is there anything else you wanted to discuss?" she asked, not looking up.

"No," Eve replied, resigned to the inevitable. "Thanks for hearing me out."

"You're welcome. Remember, my door is always open."

A thick heaviness settled over Eve as she left Brianne's office. Her dream assignment had become her worst nightmare.

Chapter Five

By 11 o'clock the next day Eve was on her fourth cup of espresso. Sleep had been elusive the night before, and the jolt of caffeine from the strong brew increased her agitation. She'd spent the morning hours before work at the local Starbucks, trying to edit story copy and put Toby out of her mind at the same time. While she'd managed to plow through a revised version of a news report, his image stubbornly remained in the back of her mind as if it was attached with super glue. By the time she arrived at the station her nerves were raw.

In her cubicle, she sat down at her desk and pored over her appointment calendar. The tinny sound of ringing telephones melded with the indistinguishable voices of the staff as they fielded phoned-in news leads.

Then the sudden shrill ring of her phone made her jump. Grabbing her cell, she pressed the on button. "Eve Norwood."

"Eve, it's Elizabeth. Sorry it's taken me so long to return your calls. I've had a full schedule lately."

"No problem. I just wanted to know if you've heard anything on those tapes you sent out."

"Relax, Eve. These things take time. I have no doubt that one of the national networks will be calling any day now. You have to trust me."

Eve switched her phone to the other ear. "I do trust you," she said, rapidly tapping her pen against the top of her desk. "It's just that . . ." How could she explain that she was in a hurry to leave Youngsville, without mentioning her problems with Toby? Elizabeth was notoriously nosy, and Eve wasn't in the mood to discuss her ex-boyfriend. "Are there positions available anywhere else?"

"There are always positions available. But I'm surprised you're asking about them now. I thought you were waiting for New York."

"Humor me."

"All right. Let me see what I've got." Eve heard the faint clicking noise as Elizabeth typed on a computer keyboard. "There's a weekend anchor job near Jackson Hole."

Eve stopped tapping. "Jackson Hole?"

"Wyoming. Fancy yourself a western girl?"

"No," she said with a grimace. "Not that I have anything against Wyoming."

A few more clicks. "There's a part-time reporter's position in Seattle."

"You know I need full-time."

"Eve, you don't sound like yourself. What's going on?"

"Nothing," she lied. "I just wanted to get an idea of the job opportunities that are out there. I think I've been narrowing my focus too much. I don't want to miss out on anything that could be right for me." She squeezed her eyes shut, hoping her agent would believe the litany of fibs rolling off her tongue.

"I really think you should wait for New York. I know what I'm talking about . . . after twenty years in this business I ought to. I have complete confidence in your talent and ability, and once the right job becomes available I'll let you know. It's all a matter of—"

"Timing," Eve finished. "I know. Thanks for looking anyway."

"You bet. But I still think there's something else bothering you." Her tone softened. "Eve, we've been through a lot together. I was there for you when Pauline died . . . you know you can tell me anything."

A sharp wave of pain sailed through her at the

mention of her mother's death. Even after a year, the grief was still fresh. And she didn't want to talk about it with Elizabeth. "Are you still planning to make a trip to Ohio?"

"Stop changing the subject," Elizabeth said sternly. "Could your bad mood have anything to do with your new series? Or that you have to work with Toby Myers?"

"How did you know about that?"

"Word gets around. You could have knocked me over with a feather when I heard he'd left the network. I'm even more surprised he took a job at his old stomping grounds. I'm sure seeing him again has dredged up a lot of old memories."

Mentally, Eve rued the day she'd confided in Elizabeth about her breakup. "I'm handling all that just fine. No problems there."

"That's good to hear. The last thing you need right now is the distraction. Keep focused on the work, Eve. No man, I don't care who he is, is worth sacrificing your career over. You're young, smart, and dedicated. I know you'll go far, I have faith in you—"

"Or you wouldn't be representing me."

"Exactly. I've got to run, but we'll be in touch."

Eve frowned as she returned the phone to its base. For the first time in her career she felt trapped, like an animal stuck in a cage with no escape.

Get a grip. She'd expended enough energy

dealing with the "Toby issue." Reaching for her planner, she crisply flipped through the pages, relieved to see her schedule provided her with plenty of other work to keep her occupied. She turned another page and glanced at the three words written on Saturday's agenda: *Bachelor/Bachelorette Auction.*

She smiled slightly. The Dreams Come True Foundation held the auction every year to benefit its charity, which assisted children with terminal illnesses. It was a cause Eve strongly supported, and this would be her second year to emcee the event. She wasn't foolish enough to actually enter it, but she'd enjoyed watching the auction unfold last year.

The wheels of her reporter's mind began to whirl. Perhaps she could turn her emcee gig into a feature story and use it as a segment for Everyday Heroes. The men and women who were brave enough to put themselves up for auction and let complete strangers bid on them certainly were heroic in her book. Maybe she could do a live feed, even.

Her thoughts screeched to a halt when she remembered she'd have to involve Toby in the report. She considered secretly lining up another cameraman to do the job, but that wasn't feasible. Besides, she wouldn't involve another employee in her scheme. Nor could she go against Brianne's edict about Toby working exclusively on the Everyday Heroes series.

She shut her day planner with a snap and tossed it on her desk. Was this what she was reduced to, contemplating sneaking behind her boss' back just so she could avoid Toby? It smacked of junior high antics, not to mention a complete lack of professionalism. What happened to her vow not to let Toby interfere with her job? But a bigger question loomed large in her mind, one that went beyond Toby's effect on her career.

When would she be free from her past?

On Friday evening, Toby sat down on the one space on his couch that wasn't covered with wrinkled clothes and mismatched bed sheets. Pushing a blue towel off an upside down U-Haul box, he propped up his bare feet on the empty carton, which was also a makeshift coffee table. He popped open a can of soda and took a long swig.

Glancing around his new efficiency apartment, he took a look at the wall-to-wall stacks of brown boxes waiting to be unpacked. His Manhattan studio had been twice as large. It would be impossible to fit everything he owned in the small, confined space that was now his home.

"Looks like it's time to downsize," he said aloud. "Can't say I'll miss this stuff." He set the burgundy pop can on the floor and surveyed the mess again. "What do you think, Jerry?"

The little gray ball of fluff had staked out his own spot next to Toby on the leather couch. He started to lift the kitten off the black cushion, but when it dug its paws deep into the expensive sofa in protest, Toby immediately let go.

Spotting the pin-sized holes the cat's razor-sharp claws left on the supple material, he knew either the claws or the costly leather sofa would have to go. "Now is that anyway to treat your hero's furniture?" he joked. "If it weren't for me, you'd still be homeless, scrounging for your supper in the garbage bins out back."

Jerry tossed him a bored look, curled up in a ball, and closed his eyes.

Toby didn't have to think twice about it—the sofa would be the first casualty. He ran a finger across Jerry's fuzzy head, causing the kitten's motor to run. Normally he didn't care much for animals. His hectic lifestyle the past several years hadn't afforded the time or energy for pets. But there was something about the small furball that appealed to him. "Well, at least you're happy," Toby said. *And at least I'm not living alone.*

He lifted his feet off the box and made a move to stand up, but his heel collided with a hard object. He glanced down and saw one of Eve's blue shoes lying on its side on the tan-colored carpet.

Toby picked it up. He'd retrieved the pair after Eve had run off. Surely the crew using the van after them had appreciated it. Carefully he'd cleaned every trace of dirt, grass and manure from both shoes, afterward buffing the leather to a soft sheen.

He remembered how angry she'd been with him. He supposed the now spotless shoes could be a peace offering of sorts, his way of making amends for inciting her fury.

Rising from the sofa, he set the shoe back on the floor and put Eve and their work out of his mind. He took another look around the new home he'd moved into two days ago, continuing to compare it with his old place. With his first paychecks from NBC he'd leased an expensive apartment in the city and filled it with trendy furnishings, stuff he enjoyed showing off to his new friends and acquaintances.

Then he was sent to Israel. After his experience there . . .

With a sharp yank he dragged another box closer to him and pulled out a cutter from his back pocket. "Time to stop stalling and get back to work," he told Jerry. Sliding the sharp blade into the brown tape, he ripped the cardboard open in one easy stroke. Reaching inside, he pulled out a gold statue, the metal gleaming in the harsh light of the shadeless lamp he'd set on the floor in the corner.

His Emmy.

Without hesitation he put the statue back in the box and closed the flaps. Lifting the heavy container, he took it to his bedroom closet, placed it on the floor and closed the door. He was in no mood to face the past tonight.

A few hours and several boxes later, Toby called it quits. A quick perusal of his refrigerator revealed two cans of pop and a takeout container of three-day-old Kung Pao Chicken. Pizza sounded more appetizing. Then he remembered the sub shop on the corner.

"Hold down the fort, Jerry." He stuffed his wallet into the back pocket of his jeans.

The kitten gave a lazy stretch.

"Guess I won't worry about you wearing yourself out while I'm gone."

The evening sun perched on the horizon, streaking the sky in pale shades of purple, pink and gold. The heat of the day had given way to a comfortable night, ideal for a short walk. It wasn't long before Toby saw the bright yellow and brown sign over the sub sandwich store. He strolled inside and headed for the counter, taking his place in line behind another customer.

Studying the menu, he had decided on his order when someone clapped him on the shoulder.

"Toby Myers! I don't believe it! What are you doing back in town?"

Toby whirled around, instantly recognizing the man behind him. "Cam Tilday!" He extended his hand out to his old friend. "How long has it been?"

Cam shook Toby's hand, pausing for a minute. "Six years, I think. Since college graduation. You haven't changed a bit. Except for this." He ran his fingers over his own smooth chin. "What's with the beard?"

Toby shrugged. "I got tired of looking at the same ugly mug in the mirror, so I thought I'd try something different." He regarded his friend and grinned. "You haven't changed . . . much."

"Don't remind me." Cam ran a hand through his thinning blond hair. "I keep telling myself it makes me look distinguished."

The line moved a few steps forward. "I thought you were still in Michigan," Toby continued. "Weren't you the one who said that once you left Youngsville you weren't coming back?"

Cam looked a little sheepish. "Michigan's a great state, but sometimes there's no place like home, you know what I mean? And what about you? I seem to recall you agreeing with me one hundred percent when I made that statement. Last I heard you were in New York working for NBC."

"How did you know that? I left after you did."

"Hey, this is a small town. It was in all the local papers a few years ago when you won that award—a Grammy, wasn't it?"

Toby chuckled. "An Emmy."

"Yeah, something like that." Cam drummed his fingers against the glass countertop. "So, are you here for a visit?"

"No, I moved back a couple of weeks ago. I live down the street now, at the Marquette Apartments."

"Can I help you?" the young woman behind the counter interrupted.

Toby faced her. "I'll take a club, extra pickles, no tomatoes, on wheat bread."

"I'll have the same," Cam said over Toby's shoulder. "Except slap some tomatoes on mine."

While she finished making their sandwiches, Cam picked up their conversation again. "Wow, six years," he said. "We have a lot of catching up to do. You'll have to tell me all about life in the Big Apple."

"Not much to tell." He wasn't ready to discuss his past, not even with a man who at one time had been a close friend. "It's all a big rat race." He pulled out his wallet as the woman rang up their order on the cash register. "It's on me," he told Cam, handing the woman a $20 bill.

"Thanks." Cam took the plastic bag that held his sandwich. They headed out of the store. "What are you up to now?" he asked, opening the door.

"Freelancing. I'm doing an ongoing series at WCBH. Next week I'm filming a couple of local commercials for a furniture store."

"Sounds interesting." Cam glanced at his watch. "Sorry to cut this short, but I have to head back to work."

Toby didn't hide his surprise as they walked outside. "On a Friday night?"

"I forgot what regular office hours were since I opened up my own practice last year," he said, a touch of weariness in his tone. "There's a lot of competition out there. Seems I'm always hustling for clients. That reminds me." He stopped in front of the sub shop window and dug in the pocket of his suit jacket. He pulled out a long, rectangular slip of paper. "A client gave a pair of these to me this morning. I was going to pass them on to someone else."

"Is that part of your hustling?" Toby joked.

"Ha ha. I hustle in a *good* way, Myers. I'm no ambulance chaser. Anyway, soon enough I'll have the clients coming to *me*." He handed Toby the ticket. "There's a dinner and an auction tomorrow night to benefit the Dreams Come True Foundation. It might be worth checking out."

"What are they auctioning off?"

Cam's grin turned wolfish. "Bachelorettes. Interested? Unless you've gotten yourself shackled to a ball and chain that won't let you out of the house at night."

Toby smirked at Cam's comment. "I'm not married," he said, then grimaced when Eve's image flitted through his mind.

"Smart man. We're too young to deal with all that commitment junk. Seems like that's all women want, anyway."

"There's nothing wrong with commitment."

Cam stuck the tip of his index finger in his ear and gave it a shake. "I must be hearing things, because I could've *sworn* that you, Youngsville's original commitment-phobe, said something positive about the evil 'c' word."

Toby shrugged. "It all depends on the woman."

"Ah, the elusive Ms. Right." Cam grinned. "Have you found her yet?"

"No . . . not yet."

"Then maybe she's just waiting for you to bid on her Saturday night." He offered Toby the ticket. "So what do you say? We can have a couple of drinks, bid on a few babes, rehash old times. And it all benefits a good cause."

"Count me in."

"Great!" Cam smiled as he handed Toby the ticket. "It starts at eight, but why don't I meet you there around seven-thirty."

Toby looked at the ticket. "It's being held at the Longhouse Building? Isn't that the crumbling old wreck the city was supposed to demolish a few years ago?"

"They fixed it up last year. Part of Youngsville's urban renewal project. It's tremendous now, one of the finest structures in the city." Cam held out his hand and gave Toby another firm handshake. "I have to get back to the office. I'll see you Saturday. Under the archway," he called out, then turned around and jogged away.

Toby stood in front of the sub shop for a few moments, watching Cam disappear down the street. He actually looked forward to tomorrow night. Even though he wasn't interested in bidding on any bachelorettes, it was an opportunity to get out of his apartment, and renew an old acquaintance. He reminded himself he could always make a donation to the foundation after the event.

Tucking the ticket into his pocket, he walked back home. He remembered Cam's prediction that he would find Ms. Right at the auction. Wouldn't that be a story to tell his grandkids?

So Grandpa, how did you meet Grandma?

I bought her at an auction.

"Yeah, right," Toby said to himself. "Like that would ever happen."

Chapter Six

On Saturday night Eve entered the Longhouse Building two hours before the auction was scheduled to start. She loved the old building, and marveled at how well it had been restored to its earlier glamour.

Walking along the crimson and gold Persian-inspired carpeting lining the lobby, she admired the cream-colored walls decorated with gold-tinted crown moldings and chair rail. The embossed high ceilings enhanced the Longhouse's grandeur. It was the perfect place to host a charity event.

When she approached the grand ballroom, she stopped and looked at the poster-sized sign leaning on an easel advertising the auction. Her gaze landed on the large photo on the bottom left corner of the placard, next to the words 'special guest.' Her photo.

Quickly she looked away. Even after four years of reporting, she was still slightly insecure watching herself on television or seeing her picture on display for the public. Except when she was previewing one of her on-air reports, she tried to ignore her image any time she saw it. Occasionally she was amazed she had chosen such a public profession, when she was basically a private person.

However, she knew why. She wanted to make a difference in the world. She *needed* to make a difference.

The crowd in the lobby had already started to thicken. Nearing the ballroom entrance, Eve accidentally bumped into a short, distinguished looking man dressed in a brown wool blazer. His salt and pepper hair was neatly combed, albeit about two decades out of style. She half expected to see a pocket protector sticking out of his jacket pocket.

"Excuse me," she said, noticing she stood at least four inches taller than him.

"Hey!" he exclaimed, his brows rising in recognition. "You're Eve Norwood, right? The news reporter?"

She smiled politely. "Yes, I am."

"Are you one of the bachelorettes?"

"I'm afraid not. I'm only emceeing the event."

"Oh," he said, appearing crestfallen. With one stubby finger he pushed his large wire-framed spectacles further up on the bridge of his nose. "That's too bad. A beautiful woman like you . . ." He suddenly turned red and gulped his drink.

She was pleased by his compliment, and slightly charmed by his obvious embarrassment. "Thank you," she said, trying to put him at ease.

"Yes, well, you're welcome." He moved aside. "I'm sure you need to get in the ballroom, since the, um, auction is starting soon. Nice meeting you." The color in his cheeks intensifying, he walked away.

Glancing at her watch, she hurried into the ballroom and surveyed the scene inside. Round tables covered with starched white cloths dotted the floor, replete with vibrant gold and red candlelit centerpieces. Tuxedo-clad waiters and waitresses flitted around making sure everything was in place. At the back of the room was a large stage with a catwalk extending from the middle of it, a podium and microphone situated stage left. Surmising that her notes and the evening's program were on the wooden stand, she started to walk toward the stage when she heard a woman call out her name.

"Ms. Norwood! Wait!"

She turned at the sound of desperation in the

woman's voice. The auction coordinator, Eloise Ruiz, bustled over to her, wearing a fuchsia, lime-green and lemon-yellow outfit. Teetering on matching high heels, the plump, diminutive woman was a whirlwind of blinding color.

She stopped in front of Eve, her ample bosom heaving slightly from the exertion of traveling across the large room. Panic filled her dark brown eyes. "Ms. Norwood, I'm so glad you're here. At least *you* showed up."

"Why wouldn't I?"

"The way my day has gone, I wouldn't have been surprised if you'd cancelled on me too." She took a deep breath. "First the chef arrives late, and we're short several trays of appetizers. Then we had an issue with the room rental. Now this."

"Now what?"

Eloise tilted her head back and looked at Eve. "You won't believe it. One of our bachelorettes has dropped out at the last minute! She told me she got engaged last night, and she didn't think it would be *appropriate* to participate in the auction." She rolled her eyes. "As if her personal life has anything to do with this."

"Don't you think she has a point? I would think her fiancé wouldn't want her going out on a date with someone else."

"But it's for charity! Doesn't she understand that? She made a commitment to do this, and she's gone back on her word." Eloise's voice grew shrill as she started to pace. "This is a disaster! The programs are already printed up. It's too late to change them. For weeks we've advertised twenty dates, but now we only have nineteen. In the five years we've held this auction, no one has ever backed out."

She paused mid-rant, bringing her hand to her chin and tapping a long neon pink nail against her bottom lip. She looked over Eve as if she was sizing up a large cream puff. "You're single, aren't you?"

Eve didn't like the direction this conversation was heading. "Yes," she replied reluctantly.

Eloise snapped her fingers and spoke in hushed tones, as if she'd forgotten Eve was standing just inches in front of her. "Why didn't I think of this before? She would be so perfect . . . she's pretty and well known—"

"Uh, Mrs. Ruiz—"

"I'm sure she'll get a very high bid. What man wouldn't want to go out with a celebrity?" She turned her attention back to Eve. "It's the perfect solution, don't you think?"

"No, I don't," she snapped. Anxiety flowed through her. Was this woman nuts? "I don't mind emceeing the auction, but I can't participate in it."

The coordinator crossed her arms over her chest, her lips pulling into a frown. "Why not?"

Eve tried counting to ten but made it only to five. "I just can't."

"That's not a reason," she said, sounding like a mother scolding a child.

The woman's blunt reply blindsided Eve. Well, why can't I? she thought. *Because it would be humiliating and degrading? Because I would appear totally desperate for a date?* She grappled for a decent excuse, convinced she must be the shallowest person on earth for having such vapid thoughts.

"Mrs. Ruiz . . ." Eve could see disappointment enter into the coordinator's eyes. Actually, it seemed more like disapproval.

"Ms. Norwood, it would only be for one night. One night and one date. Think about all the ill children our foundation benefits. We make their last wishes and dreams come true. Would you deny them that?"

Eve sighed heavily. "You're good," she muttered. "You've got me wading up to my neck in guilt."

The coordinator's eyes lit up. "So you'll enter the auction?"

As if I have a choice. "All right. I'll do it."

"Wonderful!" Eloise exclaimed with a smile. "I knew you wouldn't let us down. Oh, this is so exciting! I have a feeling tonight will be special. Very special."

While Eloise walked away, Eve's stomach turned inside out. She rushed into the lobby and found the restroom. She cupped her hands beneath the automatic spout and splashed cold water on her face. Blotting her cheeks dry with a brown paper towel, she stared in the mirror, noting the pale tone of her skin, her cocoa-colored business suit only augmenting her pallor.

Why did participating in the auction bother her so much? All the other men and women had volunteered for this, so the whole thing wasn't that big a deal. She reminded herself it was all for a worthy cause. *That* was the most important thing. And even though Mrs. Ruiz's tactics were pretty lowbrow, the woman cared about the foundation and the children benefiting from it.

She crumpled up the paper towel and tossed it in the trash can. Was it pride that made her feel this way? Was she really so vain that she cared what a roomful of total strangers thought about her social life?

No, those weren't the real reasons.

To tell the truth she was anxious. She hadn't been on a date since her relationship with Toby ended. Not because she hadn't been asked, but because she hadn't wanted to. At first she'd been too distraught over Toby's leaving. She'd thrown herself into her career, and she hadn't had much free time. And after her mother's death, she just lost interest. Besides, turning down dates had allowed her a measure of control in her personal life. Actually it was one of the few things she *could* control.

But in a few short hours she would be auctioned off to a man she'd never met, one she didn't know anything about. Then the situation would be totally out of her hands, and she would be helpless to do anything about it.

Taking a deep breath, she tried to analyze her predicament rationally. After all, this was just another part of her job. Being involved in these kinds of public events was a necessary component of her chosen occupation, she'd known that going in. So what if the agenda had changed a little? She was flexible . . . she could handle it. She was a pro.

But lately her personal life had been spilling into her professional one too much. *Way* too much.

Chapter Seven

For the umpteenth time since he'd left his apartment, Toby tugged at his necktie. The confining strip of silk fabric felt like a noose around his neck. He rarely wore the stupid things, preferring casual dress. But he'd figured at this kind of charity event the dress code would be more formal. Judging by the group of people milling outside the large building, he'd guessed correctly.

Crossing the parking lot, he approached the archway of the Longhouse. He had to admit he was impressed. The city had done a first-rate job of renovating it.

It didn't take him long to find Cam, who was leaning against one of the massive white columns that lined the front of the building.

Unlike Toby, he looked completely at ease in an expensive designer suit and geometrically patterned tie. Bringing the brown tip of a cigarette to his lips, Cam inhaled, then exhaled three flawless smoke rings, a talent he had perfected in high school.

"Still killing yourself with those things?" Toby said when he reached Cam's side. His tone was light, but inside he was disappointed Cam had continued the unhealthy habit.

Cam turned to Toby and gave him a half-hearted smile. "I need to quit." He ground out the cigarette in the large concrete urn that served as an ashtray. A flicker of regret passed over his features. "Easier said than done, though."

Toby regarded him, puzzled by his friend's uncharacteristically pensive mood. Cam had been the class clown in school, always good for a joke and a laugh, but rarely did anyone take him seriously. No one had been more surprised than Toby when Cam had announced he was interested in studying law and entering such a staid profession. It hardly seemed to fit his wisecracking personality.

But his friend wasn't wisecracking now. Which left Toby wondering if there was something deeper going on with him.

Abruptly Cam seemed to rebound, all traces of his previous glum mood vanishing. He flashed Toby a wide grin. "We're wasting time out here.

Let's go inside. I'm eager to see who's on the bachelorette menu tonight."

As they entered the Longhouse, he made a mental note to try to bring up the subject with Cam later.

Filtering through the crush of people that populated the lobby, Toby noticed how well-attended was the event. The ballroom doors were still closed, and the steady hum of conversation filled the air as waiters circulated around the room, carrying massive silver trays filled with hors d'oeuvres. Along the long wall of the lobby were several bars where people could order drinks. Cam tipped his head in the direction of one. "Want something?"

"No thanks."

Cam lifted an eyebrow. "The drinks are free," he reminded him.

"Maybe later."

"Okay. I'll be right back."

While Cam faded into the thickening crowd, Toby looked around the foyer again. He took a step backward and glanced up at the fancy engraved ceiling, halting when he accidentally jostled someone.

"Sorry," he said, casting a look over his shoulder to see who he collided with.

"I'm not."

Surprised, Toby whirled completely around. A

tall, strikingly beautiful brunette wearing a slinky red dress looked directly at him. "You can bump into me anytime," she said, moving toward him, stopping only when her arm brushed against his. Leaning forward, she brought her lips close to his ear. "Are you bidding tonight?"

Surrounded by a cloud of her cloying perfume, the flowery scent was so overpowering he had to take a step back. She was pretty, but from the smoldering way she looked at him, he could tell she was trouble. "I hadn't planned to," he answered honestly.

A slight frown tugged at her glistening red lips. "Too bad." She leaned in closer. "If you change your mind, I'm ten," she whispered.

"Pardon me?"

"My auction number," she cooed. "I'm also a ten among other things, if you know what I mean." Giving him a seductive smile, she ran her fingertip boldly down his bearded cheek as she glided past him. Within seconds she melted into the crowd.

Cam came up behind him, a soft drink in his hand. "It didn't take you long to start circulating. The two of you looked real cozy there. Who is she?"

Toby rubbed his chin where the woman had touched it. "One of the bachelorettes."

"Guess I know who you'll be bidding on tonight."

Although she was beautiful, Toby wasn't interested. "You're welcome to her."

"I don't know. She looked pretty set on you." He grinned. "Wonder if she has a friend?"

The doors to the ballroom opened and the crowd started funneling into the room. Toby and Cam followed the crush of people.

As they neared the entrance, Cam let out a low whistle. "I didn't know she was here," he said, nudging Toby in the ribs. "I'd bid on her in a second. Too bad she's just the emcee."

"Who?" Toby asked.

"Her." He pointed to the large sign outside the ballroom door.

Toby glanced at the sign, and his mouth fell open when he realized who Cam was referring to. He stared at Eve's picture, the mere image of her gorgeous smile wreaking more havoc on his system than the woman in red could ever hope to.

For a brief moment he shocked himself by agreeing with Cam, a part of him wishing Eve was doing more than emceeing the auction. Not that he would bid on her. She'd probably never speak to him again if he did.

"She's one lovely lady," Cam commented.

"Yeah, she's a hot mama, all right."

Hot mama? Toby glanced at the man standing

next to him. In his tweed jacket, wide striped tie and over-sized John Denver-inspired glasses, he appeared to be stuck in some kind of time warp.

"She's as gorgeous in person too," the man continued.

Cam leaned forward. "You know her?"

The man pushed up his slipping glasses. "I just talked to her a minute ago. Those eyes . . ."—he wiggled his graying brows—"and those legs . . . wow!"

Toby ground his teeth. The guy reminded him of one of his geeky professors from college. The man's bravado was out of line. He was acting as if Eve was a slab of prime rib and he was a starving hyena.

"I'd pay anything to go out with her," he told Cam, a lascivious glimmer in his eyes. "Money's no object."

"I hear you," Cam said with a grin, making Toby want to punch both their lights out.

Instead he yanked on Cam's arm. "Let's go." He shot the man a hostile glare before threading through the crowd.

"What's your problem?" the man called out.

Toby ignored him.

"What was all that about?" Cam asked as they entered the ballroom. "You looked ready to cream that little guy."

"Forget it."

Cam gave him an odd look. "Hey man, whatever you say." He glanced around. "Nice setup they've got here. Should be an interesting night, don't you think?"

"Yeah," Toby replied, glancing over his shoulder to see where the man went. "I'm sure it will."

The majority of the auction progressed without a hitch. At the beginning of the event butterflies continued to flit around Eve's stomach, but as the evening wore on they diminished. Keeping her focus on her notes and making sure she didn't stumble over words, she didn't pay too much attention to the bachelors and bachelorettes being auctioned off. Everyone was a sea of faceless, nameless people, and maintaining that distance helped her keep her mind from thinking about her own turn as a bachelorette. With fairly steady fingers she adjusted the curved podium microphone, preparing to introduce the final bachelor.

"Okay, ladies, here's your last chance," she said cheerily. "Introducing bachelor number ten . . . Alfred Minnefield."

Her stomach suddenly lurched as she heard chuckles ripple through the crowd. Had she made a mistake in pronouncing his name? Glancing up from her notes, she breathed a small sigh of relief when she realized the source of their laughter.

Alfred Minnefield was old enough to be her grandfather.

The diminutive Mr. Minnefield shuffled toward the middle of the stage, assisted by a gold-tipped cane. He was dressed to impress, a black silk top hat perched jauntily on his head, his tuxedo hanging a bit loose on his slight frame. He shot Eve a brilliant smile, the teasing glint in his eyes apparent behind the thick lenses of his glasses. Clearly he didn't take himself seriously, which made him that much more entertaining. She couldn't help but laugh along with the rest of the crowd. She was also grateful he appeared to have all of his teeth. Or at least he possessed a good set of dentures.

Eve read his bio as he slowly made his way down the catwalk. "Mr. Minnefield is a retired postal worker, having worked for the USPS for over thirty years. His hobbies include playing bridge and tending his garden, and of course, taking afternoon naps." She stifled a giggle as Alfred playfully tipped his hat to the approving crowd. She relaxed a little more, enjoying the way the elderly man worked the room.

"While Alfred admits his bungee jumping days are over, he can offer his date a nice dinner, good conversation, and possibly a challenging game of cards." Eve looked up from her notes. "I'm ready to take opening bids."

"One hundred dollars," a middle-aged woman shouted from the back of the room.

"Two hundred!" a svelte, young blond countered.

"Five hundred!"

The bidding continued for a few moments. Finally the last bid came in. "Sold, for seven hundred and fifty dollars," Eve said, writing down the amount next to his name. An auction volunteer would take care of getting the pertinent information from the bidder.

Eve glanced up from the podium and looked in the direction of where the final bid came. A slender blond woman in a sleek black dress daintily waved her fingers at Alfred. The audience erupted into laughter and applause, Alfred clapping along with them enthusiastically. He seemed delighted with the amount he'd brought—and with his date. He gave Eve a wink as he left the stage.

Watching Alfred disappear offstage behind the black curtain, the anxiety she'd successfully stemmed so far began to emerge. Her mouth went completely dry. Somehow during the evening she'd managed to block out the fact that as emcee she would have to auction off *herself*. How could she possibly do that, when her tongue felt like a dried out piece of shoe leather?

She stared at the group of people in front of her. They were seated at the round tables, their faces blurring as they looked at her expectantly. Perspiration broke out on her forehead and palms as desperation welled up inside of her. *Get it together, Eve.*

Then Eloise Ruiz nudged her gently, until Eve moved away. Relief passed through her as the woman flashed an encouraging smile. Eloise grasped the microphone and pulled it toward her; her head and shoulders barely cleared the top of the podium.

"Ladies and gentlemen, we have a special surprise in store for you tonight," she began. She raised her voice as murmurs filtered throughout the audience. "Please mark bachelorette Jasmine McDonald off your program. Instead, we will be auctioning off our very own emcee. Introducing bachelorette number ten . . . Eve Norwood."

A wave of applause flowed through the crowd, but Eve remained frozen in place, her feet refusing to move. Only when Eloise gave her a small but firm push from behind did Eve start walking on unsteady legs toward the catwalk.

"As you all know, Ms. Norwood is a reporter for WCBH, Channel Seven . . ."

Eloise's voice faded into the distance as Eve moved closer to the edge of the stage. She forced herself to look at the audience and form a tight-lipped smile.

"I'm ready to take opening bids," she heard Eloise say in the background.

"Five thousand dollars," a stranger's voice shouted above the murmuring crowd.

Eve's head whipped to her left, her mind jolted by the size of the bid. After a rapid search of the crowd, she saw the short man she'd run into in the lobby before the auction. He sat at one of the tables close to the stage. She expelled a heavy sigh of relief, knowing the shy man was harmless. With a tentative tip of his drink, he gave her a bashful smile.

"Five thousand dollars!" Eloise squealed, sounding like she was gasping for air. "What an opening bid! Anyone want to raise?"

Five thousand dollars! The amount ping-ponged in Toby's head. He glanced across the room at the man who made the bid, not surprised to see he was the same one who had been sizing up Eve's "assets" earlier.

Toby and Cam were also sitting near the front of the room, and they had enjoyed Eve's emceeing of the event. He had just gotten over his initial shock of her participation in the auction when the nutty professor over there decided to make that outrageous bid.

Pushing his chair back until he had a direct

view of the other man, he watched as he lifted his drink in a salute to Eve. Toby didn't miss his leering grin or his predatory expression. He knew exactly what the guy expected to get for his five thousand bucks.

"Too rich for my blood," someone from the back room shouted, causing everyone to break out in laughter. Toby remained solemn as he kept his attention on Eve, impressed with her poise on the catwalk. She came across as calm and confident, and completely unsuspecting of the jerk's motivation for bidding on her.

Without thinking he shouted out a bid. "Fifty-one hundred!"

He tried to ignore the astonished response of the audience. However, he couldn't ignore Eve's astounded look when she realized he was bidding on her.

"Fifty-five," the man countered. Remembering his comment about money being no object, Toby wanted to wipe the smug look right off his face.

"Fifty-six," Cam interjected jovially. The crowd voiced its approval.

"What do you think you're doing?" Toby snapped.

"Joining in the fun. This auction's finally getting interesting. Besides, I wouldn't mind going out with Eve Norwood. What a babe." He stood up. "Make it fifty-seven."

He jerked on Cam's arm. "Sit down!" His tone was venomous. "Six thousand," Toby called out, his stomach churning.

Cam sat back in his seat, holding his hands up in surrender. "Sorry, Toby . . . I didn't realize you wanted her that much."

"Sixty-five," the other man said without missing a beat.

Toby swallowed. "Seven thousand."

As if noticing him for the first time, the other bidder turned and faced Toby. He shot him a questioning look. Toby glared back unflinchingly.

"Seventy-five," the man said.

"Eight thousand," Toby countered, his hands balling into fists. He looked up at Eve, noticing her complexion had turned ashen. She stared at him. "What are you doing?" she mouthed, her eyes wide as saucers.

"Eighty-five," the man shouted.

Surmising that the bidding could continue like this indefinitely, Toby decided to end it. He wouldn't let Eve be subjected to this guy, no matter the cost to his bank account. From the pinched look on her face he could tell she was upset. He knew she would understand once he explained it to her later. "Ten thousand!" he declared confidently.

A collective gasp sounded from the audience.

Chapter Eight

Eve appeared sufficiently shocked. Even the other bidder looked a little off kilter. The auctioneer who had taken Eve's place sounded as if she was about to faint with glee.

"Ten thousand dollars!" she chirped, gripping the podium for support. "The highest bid of the night by far!" She looked at the other man expectantly. "Do you care to raise?"

Seconds seemed to drag into hours as the man's gaze darted from Eve to Toby, and back to Eve again. Finally, he shook his head and sat down, silently accepting defeat.

"Sold for ten thousand dollars!" The auctioneer joyously scribbled something down on a piece of paper. "Ladies and gentlemen, that ends our auction for the evening. Thank you *so* much for your support," she said, singling out Toby in particular. "Your generosity will greatly enhance the quality of life for the terminally ill children in our area. Now, feel free to enjoy the rest of your evening. There are plenty of hors d'oeuvres, and in a few minutes we'll have dancing. Also, could we have all the bachelors, bachelorettes, and the auction participants up on stage, please? We'd like to give you the chance to meet your dates."

While people rose from their seats and milled around the ballroom, Cam tugged on Toby's arm, demanding his attention. "Ten thousand dollars? Are you crazy? That's one expensive date."

"It's for a good cause," he mumbled, the reality of what he'd done only now sinking in. The check he'd have to write in a few minutes would wipe out almost all of his savings. He looked at Cam. "I wasn't about to leave her at the mercy of that creep."

"What creep?"

"The one that bid for her." Toby nodded toward the man. "You know, the guy you were talking to before the auction started. Weren't you paying attention to the things he said about Eve?"

"As far as I can tell, all he did was compliment her." Cam looked at the man, who was now talking to a group of pretty women. "He doesn't seem too broken up by losing out on her, either."

"I know what I heard," Toby insisted. *And what I saw.* He remembered the ravenous way the man looked at Eve. "It was obvious he was after only one thing."

"I think your imagination is working overtime. Or," Cam added with a knowing look, "you were jealous."

"Hardly." He had merely done a favor for a co-worker, and benefited a charity to boot. He had nothing to be jealous of.

Or did he?

He turned to the stage and saw Eve. She was still standing at the end of the catwalk, the other bachelors and bachelorettes surrounding her. He met her gaze and smiled, figuring she'd be pleased he spared her a date with a lecherous jerk.

She glared in return.

His spirits sank. Maybe he'd made a mistake after all.

Cam gestured to the stage. "You better get on up there and meet your date."

Toby looked at him, not in any hurry to face the wrath of Eve. Especially when he'd have to tell her there wouldn't be any date. Of course he'd write the foundation a check for the amount he'd agreed on. Besides, from her stormy expression, he was certain she wouldn't be interested in going out with him either.

"Don't worry about me," Cam added cheerily. "I think I'll go mix in with the crowd. Who knows, maybe I'll even find myself a date." He smirked. "For *free*."

"Very funny," Toby replied. Both men stood up, and out of the corner of his eye he saw a small, brightly dressed woman hurry over to him. He recognized her as the lady who had auctioned off Eve. She waved her hand in his direction.

"Wait!" When she reached him, she thrust out her hand. "I'm Eloise Ruiz, the coordinator of this year's auction. I just wanted to thank you personally for your generous donation, Mr.—"

"Myers," he replied, shaking her hand. "Toby Myers."

"Mr. Myers, you can't imagine how much this means to our foundation." Her pink-lipped grin stretched from ear to ear.

"I bet it does," Cam said under his breath.

Toby threw Cam a warning look before turning his attention back to Mrs. Ruiz. "It's my pleasure. I don't mind spending money on a good cause."

The coordinator glanced up at Eve, who had started to move away from the end of the catwalk and toward the middle of the stage. "I'm sure you'll be pleased with your date package and with

Ms. Norwood. We really appreciated her participation in the auction. Even if she did take just a
tiny bit of convincing," the woman added in a con-
fidential tone. "But I think you two make a mar-
velous couple." She looked at him thoughtfully
for a moment, then at Eve again. "Don't ask me
why, because I'm not sure myself, but I have a
feeling you and Ms. Norwood were meant to be
together."

"Yeah, and it only took ten thousand dollars to
make it happen," Cam quipped.

Toby hooked his elbow into Cam's side.

Mrs. Ruiz smiled and jerked her head in Eve's
direction. "I'm sure you don't want to keep Ms.
Norwood waiting."

"Maybe you better warn her in advance," Cam
joked. "This guy's not as harmless as he appears."

A peculiar expression crossed her features as
she looked from Toby to Cam, then back to Toby
again. "Well, yes," she said, stepping back, as if
she wasn't sure how to take Cam's comment.
"Again, thank you so much, Mr. Myers." Then,
like a colorful whirling dervish she scurried away
to another part of the ballroom.

He turned and glared at Cam, annoyance churning within him.

"Lighten up. You're supposed to be having
fun." The smile slid from Cam's face. "There's
something you're not telling me."

Toby hesitated for a moment. "Eve's my ex-girlfriend."

"You're joking, right?" He looked to Eve, then back at Toby. "You're not joking. Why didn't you say anything before?"

"Because it's a long, complicated story. And it's over between us. It has been for a long time." A river of regret suddenly flowed through him, catching him off guard. Questions bombarded his mind, ones he hadn't really given serious thought to until now. What if he hadn't run scared from their relationship? What if he had put someone else's feelings before his own back then? What if—

He halted his thoughts. There was no point in speculating about the past, especially now. Not when he had enough to deal with in the present.

Cam's face pinched into a baffled look. "Are you trying to get back together with her?" he asked.

"No!" Toby answered quickly. "Why would you think that?"

"Well, the fact that you just spent ten thousand dollars to go out on a date with her kind of clued me in."

"That was for charity."

"Right," Cam drawled. "You weren't so charitable to any of the other gals. I don't recall you bidding on a single one."

"Look, you can believe what you want, but I have my reasons for what I did."

"Fine. You don't want to talk about it. I get the point. Don't worry, I'll back off."

Sensing he'd offended his friend, Toby softened his tone. "Cam, it's nothing, really. Eve and I used to date, but believe me, it's over."

"No hope of you getting back together?"

"Not in this century. Ironically enough, we work together at WCBH now."

"That freelancing job you mentioned?"

"Yeah." Toby let out a self-deprecating laugh. "I really did think that guy was up to something. Guess I misread him."

"Maybe," Cam said slowly. "Maybe not. In any case, you were protecting a co-worker. I have to say, Myers, I'm a little stunned. I didn't think you had it in you."

Toby furrowed his brows. "Had what in me?"

"An unselfish streak. The Toby I used to know wouldn't have spent ten dollars, much less ten thousand, on a woman he had no intention of scoring with."

"Things are different now."

"I can see that." A contemplative look shaded Cam's features.

For the second time that night, Toby sensed there was something going on with his friend. "Is everything all right?"

Cam perked up immediately. "Everything's fine." He swept his arm in a wide arc. "There's a bevy of babes here, and I'm unattached." He grinned. "I've got the life of Reilly, Toby my man."

Toby wasn't so sure about that.

"Speaking of gorgeous women, you better meet yours." Cam pointed his thumb at the stage. "You don't want to keep her waiting."

"I don't think she's too happy with me right now." Glancing over his shoulder, he caught her blade-filled look aimed squarely in his direction. *Oh boy.* He'd definitely made an expensive mistake. "I better go straighten things out."

"Well, you've always been a smooth talker with the women. I'm sure that silver tongue of yours will get you out of this jam." He picked up his empty drink glass. "Give me a call sometime— we'll have to get together again."

"You bet."

"I wish you luck, my friend. From the daggers she's shooting you, I think you'll need it."

Toby watched Cam walk away, all the while wracking his brain trying to figure out how he was going to explain to Eve his reasoning for spending $10,000 to go on a date that would never happen. "No, buddy," he muttered. "I'll need more than luck. I'll need a miracle."

Chapter Nine

Out of the corner of her eye, Eve kept tabs on Toby as he conversed with the wiry blond-haired man who had sat next to him during the auction. Her body and mind went on auto pilot as one by one people came up to her, asking for her autograph or waiting to have their picture taken with her.

The aftershocks of what had just happened moments ago reverberated through her. *Ten thousand dollars! Is he insane? What was he thinking? Why is he even here?*

Someone shoved a rose-colored cocktail napkin and ink pen at her. Cordially she accepted it, scribbling her autograph on the fragile paper while keeping a visual on Toby. He turned slightly toward her and their gazes met. She detected the uncertainty in his eyes. In response, her own eyes thinned into small slits. He instantly broke the contact.

Good, she thought, stopping to pose for a quick picture with Alfred Minnefield and his beautiful date. Let Toby be uncomfortable. He couldn't be any more disconcerted than she was at that moment. He'd had his chance with her four years ago, and he blew it. Why was he paying an exorbitant amount of money to go out with her now?

Completely baffled, she didn't even flinch when Alfred went on tiptoe and gave her a shaky kiss on the cheek. "You're quite a gal, Ms. Norwood," he said, his smile deepening the creased lines on his face.

Eve blinked, her mind coming back into focus. "Well, thank you, Mr. Minnefield. I'm flattered."

"Any man willing to pay ten thousand dollars for a chance to go out on a date with you . . ." He gave her a crafty wink. "Like I said . . . quite a gal."

"Let's go, *Alfie,*" his date said, her high-pitched voice bordering on a whine.

Alfred elbowed Eve lightly as he tilted his head in the direction of his date. "She's quite a gal, too, don't you think? I'm right with ya, honey."

At that point Eve didn't know whether to laugh at the absurdity of her situation, or cry at the hopelessness of it. Although Mr. Minnefield's teasing had been good natured, it hit a bitter note within her. She hated not knowing Toby's motives. She also hated that she didn't have a choice in the matter. She'd been bought, and shortly she would be paid for. Despite knowing it was all for an excellent cause, she didn't feel very good about it.

"Ms. Norwood?"

Eve turned to see a young woman approaching her, wearing a blue and white badge that said VOL-UNTEER. She handed Eve a white envelope. "Here's your date package," she said with a smile. Her silver braces glinted under the bright stage lights. "I think you'll be happy with it. We managed to get several of the community's restaurants and businesses to provide their services for free. I don't know how Mrs. Ruiz does it."

"I do," Eve muttered.

"What did you say?"

"Never mind." Eve clenched the envelope in her hand. "Thanks."

"You're welcome. I hope you enjoy your date."

After Eve signed her last autograph, she looked back at Toby's table. It was empty. Briefly she scanned the ballroom, but he didn't seem to be anywhere in sight. Spinning on her heel, she walked away from the edge of the catwalk and headed toward the back of the stage, then stopped abruptly when she saw him.

Standing near the edge of the black velvet curtain, he was waiting in the wings. He'd held back from the rest of group, courteously allowing her the extra time she needed to mingle with her fans.

From his leaning stance, she figured he'd been there for quite a while. His hands were shoved into his pockets and for the first time she noticed he wasn't wearing his usual blue jeans and polo shirt. In crisp black pants, a burgundy dress shirt and black tie, he looked devastating. Just what she needed right now. For him to be courteous *and* gorgeous.

A deep and intense attraction flared within her, but she suppressed it immediately. Her body's traitorous reaction to him only served to stoke her irritation. Once again, she wondered if he had completely lost his mind. But by the looks of him, all handsome and unbelievably *calm*, he appeared the furthest thing from a lunatic.

Several different ideas for how she could get out of the date ran through her mind. The last thing she wanted to do was go on a date with Toby. She didn't spend the last four years of her life expelling him from her heart and soul only to end up having to be alone with him in a capacity that wasn't work related.

Then she thought about her reputation. Refusing the guy who had spent that amount of money would appear petty and shallow to anyone on the outside. They wouldn't understand her reasoning, even if she wanted to explain it. She had no choice—and she was totally ticked that Toby had put her in this situation.

Eve took a deep breath, fighting her rising emotions. She would handle this date thing just like any other part of her job. It would simply be another PR event. By the time she approached him, she had completely convinced herself. Lifting her chin, she determined to make the best of the situation.

To her surprise, he met her halfway in the center of the stage. A few of the auction participants and their dates still lingered around, but most everyone had already left.

"Eve—"

"Toby—"

They said their names together, and then they both paused. A partial smile played at the corners of Toby's mouth, but the emotion didn't reach his eyes. A flash of shock ran through her as he grasped her hand. "Eve, I need to tell you something."

She would have bet a week's vacation in the Bahamas she heard him gulp.

"This was all a mistake," he said in a rush. "A big huge, mistake."

Eve reacted pretty much the way he expected. First, she dropped his hand as if it had given her third-degree burns. Then her eyes grew round before narrowing into tiny slits. That caused her brows to furrow and her mouth to tighten, while her skin turned a remarkable shade of red. She looked like a bottle rocket ready to blast off.

Yep, just what he expected.

"Let me get this straight," she said in a low and menacing tone. "You just spent ten—ten—"

"Ten thousand dollars?" he supplied.

"Ten thousand dollars," she repeated, sounding even angrier than before. Which he thought would have been impossible. "All that money to win a date with me, and now you're saying you made a mistake? What kind of game are you playing?"

"It's not a game," he insisted, shoving his hand in the pocket of his pants. He rattled his keys for a moment, trying to think of what to say next. Where was his silver tongue when he needed it?

"Then enlighten me."

At that moment he knew he had no choice but to tell her the truth. As humiliating as it would be. "I might as well start at the beginning. I ran into an old friend of mine, Cameron Tilday, outside the sub shop last night. He had an extra ticket to the auction, so I figured since I had nothing better to do, I'd come here."

Eve lifted a brow. "Fascinating."

Toby ignored her sarcasm. "Believe me, I had no intention of bidding on *anyone* tonight. Until . . ."—he jiggled his keys faster—"I thought that other guy was trouble. I'd overheard him say something before the auction—"

"About me?"

"Yes, about you." He tunneled his free hand through his hair.

"I suppose it wasn't very flattering."

"Oh, it was flattering, all right. A little *too* flattering, if you know what I mean."

She regarded him for a moment, as if she was digesting what he'd said. Finally, she spoke. "You were *saving* me, is that it? Protecting me from that man who looked like he'd cry if he accidentally stepped on a spider?"

"I know it sounds crazy, but you didn't hear what he said."

She tilted her head sideways, her lips pursed tightly together. "Just to let you know, I ran into that same man before the auction started."

Whoops. Toby stilled his hand, quieting the keys in his pocket.

"And he was very courteous. And shy. And extremely non-threatening."

"Eve—"

"And even if he was a jerk, or a letch, or whatever you thought he was, I can handle myself. I hardly needed the knight-in-shining-armor routine."

Curling his hand around his keys until he felt the jagged metal edges dig into his skin, Toby fought for patience. He even prayed for tolerance.

But at that moment he realized he'd spent $10,000 in an effort to protect her from what he perceived as a threat, and all he'd gotten for his trouble were insults.

"I don't need the whiny-princess routine either," he said, not bothering to hide his annoyance. "Now, I'm going to go write my check and give it to that Christmas ornament of an auctioneer over there. Then I'm through with this. Like you said, you can handle yourself." He turned and started to walk away.

Her haughty attitude diminished immediately. "Wait," she said, placing her hand on his arm. "You can't leave it like this. What about our date?"

"Date? Eve, I wouldn't go out on a date with you if you paid *me* ten thousand dollars."

Her countenance fell, and he suspected he'd gone too far. When he saw her blue eyes grow misty, he knew he had.

"Fine," she said, squaring her shoulders despite the catch in her voice. "Now that you've made your feelings perfectly clear, I suppose there's nothing more to say."

There was a lot more to say, and he knew it. But he remained silent. He was tired of apologizing, tired of drowning in guilt, tired of saying and doing the wrong thing every time he and Eve were in the same room.

The stage was empty now. She waited a few

seconds, but he stood his ground, his heart turning to stone. Yet he felt it crumble into dust at her next words.

"You'll never change, Toby Myers," she said in a hoarse whisper. "Deep down you're still the same bum that ditched me four years ago."

Her words became his wake-up call. "Eve—"

She held up her hand to silence him, and tilted up her chin. With all the poise and grace that she effortlessly possessed, she slowly turned and headed for the stairs, as if they had just finished talking about the unpredictable fall weather or if the Cleveland Browns would ever make it to the postseason. No bystander would have suspected the two of them had shredded each other to bits with their words. She left him standing on the stage alone.

And he'd never felt so alone in his life.

Chapter Ten

The shrill ring of the telephone pierced through Eve's fitful sleep. Opening one eye, she looked at the alarm clock: 1:00. It took her a few seconds to realize she'd slept the morning through. Which wasn't too surprising. She'd hardly slept at all last night after the auction.

She picked up the receiver on the fifth ring. "Hello?"

"Ms. Norwood?"

"Mrs. Ruiz?" She sat straight up in bed and brought her fingertip to her aching temple, where a headache was starting already. Why was this woman calling her now? Eve had had enough of her and the dumb auction to last a lifetime.

91

"I'm sorry to be calling you at home. I hope I didn't interrupt anything."

Forcing herself to be polite, Eve replied, "No, not at all."

"Oh good," Eloise cooed in her usual effusive way. "I was just wondering if you'd had the chance to check over your date package. I wanted to make sure everything was acceptable."

Eve frowned. She definitely found the idea of going out with Toby unacceptable, but she didn't dare say that to Eloise. Reaching for the white envelope she'd tossed on her nightstand, she tried to think of an excuse as to why she'd have to back out of her commitment, other than telling her that Toby had ended the date before it even started. *What a jerk.* "Mrs. Ruiz, about this date—"

"I've decided to hold a small celebration in honor of our bachelors/bachelorettes and their dates, for making last night truly outstanding. I booked a dinner cruise on the *Nautica Queen* a week from this Friday." For the first time Eloise paused in her monologue. "Ms. Norwood? Are you still there?"

"I'm here," Eve replied tentatively. "I need to—"

"Don't you think that's a wonderful idea? And I also thought since you and Mr. Myers both work for WCBH—"

"Wait a minute," Eve interjected. "How did you know that?"

"He wrote it down on his donor form. If I didn't

know any better I thought you two would have planned this, except Mr. Myers couldn't have possibly known that you were a last-minute replacement. It was sweet of him to bid so much money on you anyway."

"Yeah. Very sweet."

"So I thought perhaps you two could do a story on the cruise, maybe interview some of the bachelors and their dates."

"And generate some free publicity for the foundation."

"Exactly!"

Eve took a deep breath. "Mrs. Ruiz, I'm not sure how that's going to work. There are local news stations in Cleveland you can contact, I'm sure they would be more than happy to cover the event."

"Oh, that's right." Eloise paused. "You and Mr. Myers will still come, right?"

"I'm not sure—"

"But you have to!" Eloise voice rose up a notch, making the pounding in Eve's head worse. "You emceed the event, you're a local celebrity. Everyone there will want to meet you and Mr. Myers."

Eve's spirits sank. She was all too familiar with Eloise's coercion tactics. "When is it again?" Eve asked dully.

"Next Friday, at seven P.M. I'll see you there!"

After hanging up the phone, Eve rose from her bed and headed straight for the medicine cabinet in her bathroom. She dry-swallowed two Tylenol and stared at her haggard reflection in the mirror. What was she going to do now?

"You better figure out a way to change his mind," she told her reflection. She leaned her forehead against the cold glass and closed her eyes. The sooner she took care of this, the better.

She went back in her bedroom and picked up the phone. Dialing information, she scribbled down Toby's number on the back of the envelope. Collecting her thoughts, she dialed the number.

"Hello?"

Eve felt a tickle inside her stomach at the sound of his voice in her ear. How could she have that reaction when all she wanted to do was strangle him? She gripped the phone. "Hello, Toby."

"Eve?"

"Yes, it's me." She stifled a groan. Could she sound any lamer? "I'd like to talk to you about last night."

"Okay."

"Can we meet this afternoon?"

"Where?"

She thought quickly. "Overton Park. In about an hour?"

"I'll be there."

"Great." She started to hang up the phone when she heard him speak again.

"Eve . . . I'm glad you called."

Fifty-five minutes after his phone conversation with Eve, Toby steered his cobalt-blue truck into the parking lot at Overton Park. The morning sunlight had given way to a cloudy afternoon sky. An elderly man walking a beagle passed in front of Toby's vehicle, but other than that the park appeared deserted.

A cherry-red Honda whipped into the space next to him. He didn't even have to look to know it was Eve. Even through the steel door barriers he could sense her presence.

He opened the door, and an oppressive wave of heat greeted him. Walking around her car, he met her on the driver's side. "Hi," he said, hooking his thumb in the belt loop of his blue jean shorts.

She grabbed her purse and shut the door. "Hi."

They stood for a few awkward moments. She seemed unsure of herself, and he wanted to put her at ease. He gestured to a nearby park bench. "Do you want to sit down?"

Nodding, she moved to the bench, with him trailing behind. They both sat down, and she started to speak, but he held up his hand and stopped her.

"Before you say anything Eve, I know I was really out of line last night. I regret some of the things I said. Well, that's not exactly true. I regret *all* of the things I said." He glanced around the park. "For some reason, I keep saying and doing everything wrong when we're together. But there is one thing I want you to know."

"And what is that?" she asked, eyeing him coolly.

"I *know* you can handle yourself. You've blossomed over the past four years. I recognize that now."

"No longer the insecure little mouse you used to know?"

"You were never mousy to me," he insisted. He remembered the shy, reserved intern she'd been when she first started working at the station. He'd been attracted to her the moment she walked into the newsroom, and had considered it a personal challenge to break her out of her shell. He realized now that she had come into her own without him. With great difficulty he resisted the urge to tuck an errant strand of her silky blond hair behind her ear. *You were always beautiful.*

The words popped in his mind before he could stop them. And they were the truth. She was even more beautiful now, her cheeks rosy and glowing from his compliment.

She averted her gaze, and this time he couldn't

ignore his inner instincts not to touch her. With two fingers he tilted her chin toward him. "Can we put all this behind us, Eve? I'm talking about all of it, not just last night. Is there any way we can start over again?"

For a long moment she didn't say anything. Then she took his hand, removing it from her face. When she let it go, he could read the vulnerability in her eyes.

"Just tell me one thing," she said.

"Anything."

She took a deep breath. "Why did you leave me?"

Chapter Eleven

Eve wanted a sinkhole to appear in the middle of the park and swallow her up. Why was she bringing their past up now? He'd suggested they start over, to put everything behind them, which was probably a good idea.

Apparently her masochistic side couldn't leave it at that.

She couldn't sweep what happened between them under the rug and hide it away. For some reason, she had to know the answer to the question that had haunted her for years.

Was she ready to handle the truth? Would he even give it to her?

To her surprise, however, Toby didn't hesitate in his answer. It was as if he'd always had the reply to this particular question ready on his lips, waiting for her to ask it.

"Because I was stupid, Eve. And selfish. And I only cared about having a good time." He paused for a moment. "You can stop me anytime, you know."

"Keep going."

"I guess self-abasement works for me."

"You said it, I didn't."

He dropped his gaze. "I saw other women while we were together."

She drew in a sharp breath. At the time she'd had an idea she wasn't his only girlfriend, but deep in the throes of her foolish infatuation with him, she'd chosen to ignore her suspicions. Having them confirmed, even years later, didn't lessen the hurt.

He lifted his eyes to her. "You were the only serious one."

"That makes me feel *so* much better," she said, unable to keep the sting from her voice.

He briefly hesitated at her comment, as if he identified with her hurt. Then he continued on. "I got scared. Scared of my feelings for you, most of all. So when I was offered the job in New York . . . well, leaving town seemed the best way to solve all my problems."

Pain scored her heart at his words. "So that's all I was to you? A problem that needed solving?"

She took a shuddering breath. "If you're trying to spare my feelings, you're doing a lousy job."

"Eve, listen to me. I don't want to fight about this. You're the one who asked, remember?"

"Yes," she admitted, thinking it was the dumbest thing she'd ever done in her life. She had to have some kind of mental defect, because she couldn't seem to keep from asking to be hurt all over again.

"I was such an idiot," she mumbled, thinking about the evening two days before he had left for New York. "We'd gone out for what, a couple of months?" She remembered how easy it had been for her to say those three simple words. The memory of him kissing her after she'd expressed her deepest feelings was still as clear as a crystal goblet. "I thought you felt the same way," she whispered. "I guess that makes me a bigger fool."

"You're not a fool. If anyone was a fool, it was me."

"I promised I would never be hurt like that again," she continued as if he hadn't spoken. *Even if it meant living with an empty space in my heart.*

"I'm sorry, sorrier than you'll ever know. To be completely honest, I was sorry I left the moment I stepped on that plane to Manhattan."

"You didn't seem to suffer too much. A job at NBC, a high-profile assignment in the Middle East. An Emmy award," she added tartly, not bothering to hide her envy.

"It had nothing to do with work, Eve. I used my job as an excuse to run away. But I want to do the right thing now, what I was too much of a coward to do four years ago." He focused on her earnestly. "Eve, I took you for granted when we were together. I also made a huge mistake when I left without giving you an explanation. Can you forgive me?"

Her shock left her speechless. Her gaze never left his, and in the brown depths of his eyes she could read so many emotions—regret, sorrow, even a layer of pain so stark it jolted her. No pride. No false sentiment. He was stripped bare, until she could nearly see inside his soul.

"Does my forgiveness mean that much to you?" she said, fighting the lump that had lodged in her throat.

"It means everything."

A thought occurred to her. "Is that why you bid for me Saturday night? Was spending ten thousand dollars your way of doing penance for the past?"

His jaw tightened. "No," he stated firmly. "I did that because I thought I was helping you out. Now I can see it just created more problems."

Eve looked away. "Ms. Ruiz called me this afternoon."

"She did?"

"Yes." She met his gaze again. "She's decided to have a 'pre-date' cruise."

"A what?"

"She wants all the winning bachelors and bachelorettes to go on an evening cruise on the *Nautica Queen*. Kind of a thank you for all the generous donations that were given at the auction. She mentioned yours in particular."

"That's just great." He leaned back on the bench and feathered his fingers through his hair. "So now we have to go on two dates?"

She gave him a sharp look.

"Okay, that didn't come out right. What I meant was we're not comfortable even going out on one date, much less two." He cast her a side-long look. "Right?"

"Right." Her tone sounded a bit unsure. "Right," she repeated, a little more forcefully this time.

"So . . ." he cleared his throat. "What do you suppose we should do?"

"Well, there's only one thing we can do. Show up. Ms. Ruiz pointed out that it would be a good press opportunity, and I have to agree with her."

"Eve, I'm perfectly willing to back out on the date. And I'll put the blame all on me. I don't want to force you to do something you don't want to do."

His chivalrous attitude was charming. And unexpected, especially coming from him. Maybe he had changed after all.

But it wasn't that simple. Nothing ever was.

"I'll be fine with it, Toby," she said, convincing herself as much as him. "Besides, it would be a great story for Everyday Heroes—reporting on the generosity of so many to help make terminally ill children's dreams come true."

"Good point." He regarded her for a moment. "It's business, then."

"Yes," she said, nodding firmly. "Just business." And she could handle being on a date with Toby that was just business.

Couldn't she?

Chapter Twelve

The next morning Eve walked into the meeting to see everyone's attention focused squarely on her. An overwhelming sense of déjà vu consumed her as she remembered this same scenario had played out the previous Monday. *So much for keeping my bachelorette experience a secret.*

"You're looking a little worse for wear," Jason Brook commented. "Heard you had a little excitement this weekend."

"It's no big deal." Pulling one of the chairs back from the table, she slipped into her seat.

"Ten thousand dollars sounds like a big deal to me. Gotta wonder how a guy like Myers has that kind of money to spend." He leaned over the table. "I didn't realize you were so expensive."

Everyone grew silent. Eve turned and looked at him. She had enough crowding her mind and she wasn't in the mood to deal with a conceited reporter's sour grapes. "I'm not expensive. Just picky."

Her co-workers broke out in a fit of laughter. Jason frowned and looked away.

Finally, she had put Jason Brook in his place.

Brianne entered the room, effectively quieting everyone down. She began discussing assignments, but it didn't take long for Eve's thoughts to wander. She and Toby would be going on a date. *A date*. The word kept replaying in her mind like a broken record. Each time, she had to remind herself that she and Toby wouldn't be on a date, they would be covering a story. But for some reason her mind wouldn't focus on that. Doodling absently on her pad, she tuned out Brianne and tried to calm the annoying butterflies that had suddenly made an appearance in her stomach.

"Eve?"

Brianne's voice penetrated her musings. "Yes?" she replied.

"Did you hear what I just said?"

Heat suffused her face. "I'm sorry. Would you mind repeating it?"

The station manager didn't try to hide her annoyance. "I wanted to know if you had anything for today's Everyday Heroes segment?"

"Um, yes," Eve said, grabbing her pad and flipping through the pages. "Across town, in Shady Grove, 4345 Vine Street."

"Who's the hero?" Brianne asked, marking down the information.

"Buster."

Baffled, Brianne stopped writing. "Buster?"

"He's a Newfoundland."

"You're doing a story on a dog?"

"Not just any dog. Buster rescued his owner's three-year-old granddaughter from their backyard pool yesterday. And the little girl's grandfather happens to be Addison Bunderstein, the mayor of Shady Grove. If he could, he'd give the dog the key to the city. He'll have to settle for his heroic pet being the subject of a news feature instead."

"Sounds good," Brianne said, nodding. "All right everyone, let's get to work!"

An hour later, Eve headed for the WCBH parking lot to meet Toby. She got her mindset into interview mode, trying to push her thoughts about Toby and their appointment with the *Nautica Queen* out of her mind. She wasn't too successful.

She felt a tap on her shoulder, which caused her to nearly jump out of her skin.

"Sorry, I didn't mean to startle you," Toby said, falling in step next to her.

That she couldn't relax in his presence was starting to wear on her. "Are you ready to go?"

"Ready as I'll ever be."

She half expected him to bring up their date on their way to the Bundersteins' but he didn't. Instead he just whistled, occasionally looking her way and giving her a small smile as if everything in his world was perfectly normal. She found herself disappointed and more than a little annoyed that he wasn't affected by this as much as she was.

A short time later they arrived at the Bundersteins' quaint bungalow. Addison Bunderstein and his wife Joan directed them to the family room, where Toby quickly got to work setting up his ENG equipment.

Eve was a few minutes into the interview with the Bundersteins when a dog the size of a small bear came bounding into the room.

"There's our hero now," Addison said enthusiastically. "Come here, boy! Make sure you get him on camera too."

"You bet," Toby said, from his position behind the tripod.

Eve couldn't say anything.

She'd never seen a Newfoundland before. Buster was huge, with a black shaggy coat and a long string of drool trailing from his mouth. When the dog lapped his tongue a few times over his owner's face, Eve thought she might lose her lunch.

"That's a good puppy." Addison gave Buster a nice scratch behind the ears.

Eve gulped. "He's still a puppy?"

Buster's ears perked. He turned his head in Eve's direction, as if he'd just noticed her presence. Then without warning he lunged at her, causing Eve to freeze with fright.

He skidded to a halt right in front of her and gave her a wet, slobbery kiss. *Ugh.*

"Oh, Ms. Norwood! He likes you," Joan Bunderstein gushed. "Buster doesn't always take to strangers right away."

"That's nice." Eve wiped doggy drool from her chin and forced herself not to end the interview right there. Buster sat back on his haunches beside her feet, his breath coming out in heavy puffs. Right in her face.

"Did you get that on film?" Addison asked Toby.

"Technically it's videotape," Toby replied, still looking through the eyepiece. Then he stepped back and looked around the camera, directly at Eve. She didn't miss the laughter twinkling in his eyes. "But yes, I got it."

"Terrific!" Addison said. "Now, where were we?"

Eve conducted most of the interview with Buster blowing his biscuit-scented breath in her face. Deciding near the end of filming that he was tired, the huge dog plopped down on the floor, directly on top of Eve's feet.

"Isn't that cute," Joan said. "He does that to my husband all the time."

"He'll be a great foot-warmer in the winter," Addison added with a laugh.

Within seconds Eve's left foot fell asleep. She tried wiggling it beneath the dog's belly in an attempt to get Buster to budge, but it was no use. He was already in canine dreamland, snoring away.

She heard Toby's deep-throated chuckle, and she shot him a scathing look. He gave her an innocent one in return.

The interview ended, and Eve had no choice but to gracelessly yank her feet from beneath Buster's belly. That earned the dog's immediate attention, and Eve another drippy kiss.

Addison stood from his brown leather recliner. "Thanks so much for coming out."

"It's been . . . interesting," Eve managed, glancing at Buster suspiciously. Rising from her seat, she looked down at her skirt. It was covered with long black hairs.

"As mayor, usually when I talk to the media it's because something's gone wrong," Addison pointed out. "It's a nice change of pace to be a part of a good news story."

"We're glad to be able to report it," Eve replied. And she was, despite Buster's unusual attraction to her. "I'm thankful your story has a happy ending."

"Just remember to remind your audience about putting fences around private pools. I'd hate to see what almost happened to us happen to another family."

"We will." She tried to discreetly brush the dog hair off her clothing while Toby started breaking down his equipment.

Addison noticed. "Sorry about that," he said. "Buster's blowing his coat right now."

"Yes," Joan added. "The breeder told us we'll have to go through this twice a year. I try to keep up with it." She shrugged. "Buster can be high maintenance sometimes."

"But he's worth it, aren't you boy?" Addison said, scratching his personal hero behind the ears.

Once they loaded up the equipment, Toby checked his watch. "It's a little after eleven," he said, winding up a cable cord. "We can get back to the station and edit the feature there." He looked at her for a moment, amusement sparkling in his eyes. "You're not used to dogs, are you?"

"What makes you say that?"

"Oh, I don't know, maybe because you looked scared out of your mind when Buster licked you."

"I'd like to see how calm you'd be if a bear lunged at you."

Toby hung the cord on a peg inside the back of the van. "He's not a bear, he's a dog. Besides, he's more like a little kid than anything else. He just wanted some attention."

"I didn't realize you were such a fan of dogs."

"Dogs are okay," he said, slamming the door shut. "I'm more of a cat person, myself."

"You like cats? I don't remember you having a pet before."

"Until a couple of weeks ago, I didn't. Then I found this kitten back behind my apartment building, and I decided to keep him. Before Jerry, I'd always thought pets were too much responsibility."

"And now?"

"Now I like the companionship. It's kind of nice to have someone—or should I say *something*—greet me at the door when I come home." He paused. "Hold still."

She inhaled sharply when he reached out his hand and lightly brushed her cheek with his fingertip. The contact sent heady currents of electricity streaking though her body.

"Dog hair," he explained, gently trailing his finger against the side of her face. She didn't miss the low, husky tone of his voice, and she watched in fascination as his eyes darkened to a smoky brown.

The attraction between them sizzled, and she was fairly sure they both felt it. A dazed expression crossed his features, mirroring her own mixed-up emotions. *What is happening here?*

She could read the unspoken question in his eyes.

"Ms. Norwood!" Joan Bunderstein called from the top of the driveway.

Eve and Toby jerked away from each other. Averting her gaze, she tugged at the bottom of her suit jacket, hoping her heated cheeks didn't look as hot as they felt. Squaring her shoulders, she struggled to blank her features before walking around to the side of the van.

"We were just leaving," Eve called out to Joan, flinching at telling the half-truth. "What did you need?"

Joan hurried to meet her. "You forgot this." She held up Eve's handbag.

"Thanks. I'd be lost without it."

"I know what you mean," Joan said. "I carry almost everything I own in mine."

Eve turned at the sound of Toby starting up the van. Was it her imagination, or was he revving the engine up a little too high? "I've got to go," she told Joan. "Thanks again for the interview."

"Our pleasure. Best of luck to you."

Toby remained silent on the ride back to the station. Tension oozed from him, and she could sense his mood had changed. Was it because of what happened in the Bundersteins' driveway? Had she had the same effect on him as he had on her?

She tried to ignore the small part of her that hoped she had.

Toby's emotions were riding as high as the van's RPMs. From the moment he'd touched Eve's cheek he'd been transported somewhere else. The Bundersteins, Youngsville, even the whole world seemed to disappear, leaving behind the beautiful woman in front of him. If Joan hadn't shown up just then he might have actually kissed. *Yeah, and that would have been real professional.*

"Did you say something?" Eve asked.

"No," he said quickly, not realizing he'd said the thought aloud.

"Oh. I guess I'm hearing things."

"I guess so."

He knew he sounded a little short, but he couldn't help it. With his thoughts and feelings all in a jumble he was surprised he could string more than two words together.

"Don't you think you're going a bit fast?"

He gave the speedometer a cursory glance. "Oh, yeah. Sorry." He slowed down.

She let out a long sigh and leaned back in her seat.

There was still so much unresolved between them. They had forged a tentatively friendly relationship, but he knew that was as far as she wanted or would let it go. Not to mention the intense emotions he'd experienced back at the Bundersteins' had been totally unexpected. But they had felt good. Real good.

He drove a few more miles, cogitating his predicament in his mind. He liked her, there was no doubt about that. And far beyond the realm of a professional relationship. He suddenly realized this was all new to him—being on the requited side of an unrequited relationship. And he didn't like it one bit.

How was that for poetic justice?

Chapter Thirteen

Eve sank against the back of the seat in the van, weariness seeping through her body. But that wasn't the only thing her body was feeling. Her mind reflected on Toby touching her at the Bundersteins'. The look in his eyes when his gaze met hers. The shiver of pleasure that had gone through her . . .

Stop! Why did she do this to herself? She looked at Toby. He was quiet, thoroughly concentrating on the road ahead. Just like he always was when he was driving. Nothing had changed.

I imagined it. What kind of desperate woman takes an innocent gesture like swiping a piece of hair and turns it into some declaration of . . . of . . . Good grief, she was confused. And tired.

And sick to death of analyzing everything. She closed her eyes and blanked her thoughts, refusing to ponder for another minute Toby and his imagined intentions.

A short while later she felt Toby nudging her with his hand. "Eve," he said softly. "We're here."

She opened her eyes to see the sandstone-brick building that housed the WCBH offices. "I fell asleep?" Self-consciously her hand went to her hair and she smoothed it down.

"Are you okay? You look exhausted."

"I'm fine," she said, unfastening her seatbelt.

"Maybe you should take the day off."

She eyed him squarely. "Toby, I've never taken a day off, and I'm not about to start now."

"Not even a vacation day?"

"Nope. I'm very dedicated to my job."

"I know that. But you need a break once in a while or you'll burn out."

"Not me," Eve said as she opened the door. "National networks aren't interested in slackers."

"So you have your eye on New York?" Toby pushed open the driver's side door.

It was much easier to talk to him when the topic turned to her career. "Of course. Doesn't everybody? *You* did," she said pointedly.

"Eve, that job pretty much fell in my lap."

She rolled her eyes. "Great. That's just what I want to hear."

"New York isn't all it's cracked up to be. The hours are long, the stress is high—"

"That doesn't bother me."

"And then there's the chance they'll tap you for an overseas job like they did me." His expression instantly clouded, and he turned and got out of the van.

Eve slid out of her seat and shut the door. She met him behind the vehicle. He had backed the van into the space and close to a tall hedge. The position secluded them from the office building and occasional passersby.

"None of that sounds bad to me, Toby," she said, continuing their conversation. "In fact, it's exactly what I want."

"Let me guess. You want more money, more prestige, and more notoriety." He ticked off each word on his fingers.

"You talk about those things as if they were bad. It's not just about money and fame. I want to make a difference in the world, Toby. I want to report on stories that can affect lives."

"You already do that. Here, in Youngsville."

"But it's not the same."

"Sure it is. You don't have to have millions of people watch you on television in order to be successful. There are needs to be filled here and in other small markets."

She squirmed beneath his scrutiny. "You act as

if you care about what I do and how I do it," she said quietly.

He paused. "I do care. I care a lot."

A part of her didn't want this, didn't want him looking at her with those incredible brown eyes, wreaking havoc with her emotions and drawing her closer to him. But another part of her longed for his tender affection. How long had it been since someone had actually *cared* for her?

But why did it have to be him? He'd wounded her so badly before. She couldn't let her defenses down, not without risking her heart again.

His cell phone suddenly rang. He whisked it out of his pocket and flipped it open. "Myers here. Yes . . . okay, we're on our way." Sliding the phone into the back pocket of his jeans, he looked at Eve. "A fire broke out on Fifty-ninth and Inde-pendence," he said briskly. "Brianne wants us to cover it."

Immediately, they both raced to the front of the van and clambered inside, putting their personal conversation on hold. Within moments they head-ed for the downtown residential area of Youngsville.

They were at least a mile from their destination when she saw thick billowing clouds of black smoke above an apartment building. Fear sudden-ly surged through her body.

Toby stopped the van near the building and

vaulted out of the seat. With expert timing he retrieved his equipment. In minutes they were heading toward the burning building.

Eve's forehead broke out in perspiration. The intense heat of the fire added to the humid and heavy summer air. Flames spewed out of a few of the windows. Two firefighters climbed an extension ladder to reach the top floors.

Wiping her damp forehead with her hand, she approached one of several police officers who were keeping the gathering crowd at bay. After getting his attention she gathered basic information on the situation so that she would at least have a preliminary report when they went live in a few minutes.

"Is there anyone still in the building?" Eve asked.

The officer lifted his hat and scratched his bald pate. "I don't think so. This is an old building. It should have been condemned years ago. There were only a few families living inside but we're confident we got everyone out."

"Mr. Police Officer?"

Eve and the officer both looked down at the same time. A young girl about five or six years old stared up at them with wide, frightened brown eyes. She was thin and her black hair was braided tightly against her scalp. She clung tightly to a dirty, half-dressed Barbie doll.

"Have you seen my momma?"

The policeman hunkered down in front of the girl. "Isn't she over there with everyone else?" He pointed to a group of people, mostly women and children, standing by one of the city's yellow fire trucks.

The girl shook her head.

"Why don't we go on over and see."

"She ain't there," the child insisted. "I already looked. I ain't seen her since she went to her room to take a nap."

"When was that?"

"Right before the firemen came and picked me up."

"Did you see them bring your mommy out?"

She shook her head again.

"Where's her room?"

Lifting her small hand, she pointed to the top floor of the building.

A knife twisted in Eve's chest as she saw the officer's complexion turn ashen. Immediately, he scooped up the little girl and dashed to the fire truck. "There's someone still in the building!"

Oh dear God. The reality of the situation hit her full force. She glanced up as more smoke and flame poured out of the tall red structure. A wave of nausea threatened to overtake her.

Hearing footsteps, she numbly turned around to see Toby striding toward her, shouldering his camera. "I'm ready for the live feed," he said, then stopped in his tracks. "Eve? What's wrong?"

"Someone's still in there." Her voice sounded hoarse. She glanced at the fire truck and immediately spotted the little girl. Although she was surrounded by people, she looked completely alone. Eve could see the shine of tears streaking the child's dark cheeks. Suddenly she felt her own slipping out of the corners of her eyes.

She didn't understand it. She'd covered her share of tragic events before. But this time it was different. She identified with that little girl, even though they had nothing in common. Nothing except loneliness . . . and the pain of losing their mothers.

With his free hand Toby reached out and grasped her shoulder, giving it a little shake. "Eve." He moved toward her until there was almost no space between them, the camera partly shielding them. "You've got to pull it together. Think about the job . . . we're supposed to be going live in a couple of minutes."

"I-I can't," she stammered, her mind filled with a myriad of images. The little girl's tears. Her own mother lying in the hospital bed as she gasped her last few breaths.

"Yes, you can. The firefighters will rescue whoever's in there." He reached for her hand, squeezing it tightly.

* * *

Toby had never seen Eve like this before. And it scared him.

When he first approached her moments ago she looked like she was in shock. Her face was gray, and she was crying. It had surprised him. Not that the situation wasn't dire, because it was. But since his return from New York she'd seemed almost emotionless, except for the times she had been angry with him. Now she appeared ready to shatter into a thousand pieces. The sight nearly shook him to the core.

But somehow she managed to pull herself together. Releasing his hand, she stepped away from him, wiped the tears from her eyes, then tugged on her suit jacket. The transformation from vulnerable woman to seasoned professional was amazing.

When they went live on the air the drama unfolded behind them. News wise, Toby couldn't have asked for a better shot. Despite the almost blinding smoke and flames that continued to consume the building, the firefighters managed to rescue the little girl's mother. He filmed one fireman as he draped the unconscious woman over his shoulder and descended down the ladder.

Adrenaline pumped through Toby. It all reminded him of the Middle East, where he had filmed dramatic rescue attempts . . . along with tragic failures.

I can't think about that now. He had to heed

the advice he gave to Eve. Focus on the job. Later he'd deal with the emotional aftermath, which he knew would come when the ordeal was over.

It always did.

For the next several minutes he and Eve continued their live report, informing their audience that the rescued woman was still alive, but was being treated for smoke inhalation. As soon as they cut back to the studio, she handed Toby the microphone. "I'll be right back," she said, then hurried toward a yellow fire truck. Puzzled, Toby balanced his equipment on his shoulder and followed her.

She knelt down beside a bedraggled little girl, talked to her for a few moments, then drew her in her arms.

He swallowed, touched by the scene.

Eve grasped the little girl's hand, and the two of them walked over to him. "This is Shauna. That was her mother they rescued."

Toby couldn't speak. He simply stared at the girl, her brown eyes peeking at him beneath thick black eyelashes. She clutched Eve's hand as if she would never let it go.

"I'm going to ride in the ambulance with Shauna and her mother," Eve told him.

He couldn't believe what he was hearing. "Eve, Brianne will want another report for the six o'clock newscast."

"Explain it to her." Eve brought Shauna closer to her. She flicked a glance at the girl and then back at Toby. "She has no one else," Eve whispered.

Toby knew Brianne would be furious with her for abandoning an assignment, especially a live one. "I'll do what I can," he said, although he had no idea what he would say. But at that moment it wasn't important. Taking care of that little girl was.

"Thanks."

"What hospital?"

"Metro," she replied over her shoulder.

"I'll meet you there when I'm done."

He half expected her to refuse, to don her cloak of independence and tell him she'd manage on her own. To his surprise, she nodded in agreement.

Toby let out a relieved breath. It seemed today was a day for miracles.

Chapter Fourteen

"Are you hungry?"

Eve slumped against the seat in Toby's truck. The sun had set over two hours ago and exhaustion seeped into every muscle she possessed. Just as he promised, he had met her at the hospital after he'd finished working, and assured her he'd smoothed everything over with Brianne. Eve wasn't totally surprised by the news. She knew if anyone could work things out with Brianne, Toby could.

Grateful she still had a job, all she wanted to do was go back to her apartment and fall into bed. "No. I don't have much of an appetite."

"I knew you'd say that." He exited the Metro Hospital parking lot and turned right onto

Sherman Avenue. "Why don't we stop somewhere on the way back to the station."

"Not tonight, Toby, all right?"

He cast a glance in her direction. "All right," he said, giving her a slight smile. "I won't force you to eat."

"I appreciate that."

They rode the rest of the way in silence.

"I'm sorry you had to go through that alone. I know it must have been tough for you."

Toby's voice withdrew her from her thoughts. "What do you mean?"

"You know . . . considering what happened to your mom . . ." His words trailed off and he stared at the road ahead. "I probably shouldn't have brought that up."

"It's okay." And for some inexplicable reason it was. Just as it wasn't as difficult as she'd thought it would be when she and Shauna sat in the emergency room waiting for news about her mother. She hadn't stepped foot in a hospital since her own mother had died. But as long as she'd had little Shauna to focus on, she didn't have to deal with the bad memories.

He pulled into the WCBH lot and parked the van. They both got out and walked to her car in silence.

"You haven't said anything for a while," he pointed out when they reached the driver's side door.

She blew out a long stream of air and turned to him. "There's nothing to say."

"Eve. Don't shut me out. I can tell you're hurting." His hand went to her cheek. "I know what it's like to lose someone."

She leaned into him, drawing comfort from his closeness, taking solace in the tenderness she saw in his expressive, dark eyes. Memories flooded her mind—*good* memories this time. Images of how they used to laugh together, of some of the talks they used to have. Of how secure she'd felt when he took her in his arms . . . and how special she'd felt when he kissed her.

The harsh fluorescent light from the parking lot lamps illuminated his gorgeous face. Their eyes locked. Eve saw his expression suddenly change, and the pressure from his fingertips increased slightly against her cheek. It was all the impetus she needed. Slowly she reached up and clasped her arms around his neck. Powerless to stop herself, she tilted her face up to his.

Toby's determination nearly dissolved the moment she put her arms around him. More than anything he wanted to draw her close, to kiss away the veil of pain and doubt in her eyes, reflecting what she surely felt in her heart. He leaned in closer, until his mouth hovered over hers. His pulse raced in anticipation of the kiss.

Then it stopped as she pulled away.

"Eve," he said, almost choking on her name. He reached out to touch her again, but she retreated even further.

"I-I'm sorry," she said. "I shouldn't have done that." She turned her back to him. "I'm tired, I didn't know what I was doing . . ."

He walked up behind her and placed his hands on her shoulders. "It's okay. I didn't mind."

"You should have."

"Eve, you're not making any sense."

She shrugged him off and faced him. "Can't you see where this is heading? We're right back where we were four years ago. It's like nothing's changed."

"No, Eve. You're wrong. Everything's different— you, me, our lives, the situation. Everything."

Shaking her head, she stepped back from him. "I can't go down this road again. We have to keep our relationship professional."

"I'm not sure we can." He looked at her intently. "And I don't think you want to."

"You don't have a clue about what I want!"

"Then tell me, Eve. What is it you want? Because your words are saying one thing, but when I look at you I see something else." He plunged his hand through his hair. "Or maybe we're both just confused."

They looked at each other for a long moment. Then she reached inside her purse and pulled out her keys. She turned around and unlocked her door. "I've got to go."

"Eve—"

"Toby, I can't deal with this right now. I can't deal with you."

"So you're running away? You think that's going to solve anything? Take it from someone who knows, escaping the problem doesn't make it disappear."

She didn't turn around. She didn't even answer him. She just got in her car and drove away.

Eve banged her fist on the steering wheel as she drove home. When would she learn? She'd made a complete fool out of herself, first practically throwing herself at him and then pulling away. No wonder he was confused and frustrated with her.

But even worse, she felt a slight bit of satisfaction that he was twisting in the wind because of her mixed signals. When had she become that type of person? She wasn't vindictive, she never had been. Sure, over the past four years she had hated him for hurting her, and had wanted him to experience as much pain as she had. But those were just thoughts, not actions. She was becoming someone she didn't recognize. Someone she didn't like at all. But she didn't know how to keep her bitterness at bay.

Pulling into the parking lot of her apartment complex, she slipped into her space and got out of her Honda. She grabbed her purse and shut the door, in a hurry to get inside. She needed time to think, time to sort out her thoughts and emotions, things she couldn't do when she was around Toby. She'd reached the sidewalk that stretched out in front of her apartment building when the screech of tires filled the air.

Turning around, she saw a dark colored truck whip into the lot and head straight for her building. The vehicle slowed down in front of her. It belonged to Toby.

The passenger's side window lowered smoothly and he put the truck in park. He slid the bench seat closer to the window. "Eve!" he called out to her. "Wait."

She halted, not realizing how relentless he could be. "How did you know where I live?"

"I followed you. You can't keep running away, Eve." He opened the door and leaped out. In two long strides he was in front of her.

"I don't need you to tell me what I can or cannot do."

"You're right. You don't." He sighed. "I guess I should have known that."

"Now that you've met your self-awareness quota, will you please leave?"

"No. Not until we work things out."

"Why can't you just leave me alone?" she blurted in frustration.

"Because I want to get everything between us out in the open, Eve. I'm tired of not dealing it. Aren't you?"

She paused for a moment and let out a deep breath. It was as if she had expelled all of her energy in that one action.

"Is there some place we can go to talk?"

She couldn't resist one more weak, sarcastic remark. "Afraid you can't trust me in my own apartment?"

"No. I'm afraid I can't trust myself."

That wasn't the reply she'd expected. And she had no response to it.

"There's a pancake house down the street."

"Pancakes at eleven at night?"

"I know it's late, but they're open twenty-four hours. I'm sure it won't be crowded right now. Not unless there's a midnight special on waffles or something."

His comment almost made her smile. *Almost.*

"What do you say?"

It was time to clear the air. She knew that in her heart more than anything. And he was right about one thing, although she'd never admit it to him. She couldn't run away anymore. This time she'd have to face her relationship with Toby straight on.

"Okay," she said, clutching her keys. "I'll meet you there."

Chapter Fifteen

Toby held the door open for Eve as they walked into the restaurant. As he predicted, the dining area was nearly empty, except for two men sitting at a bar drinking coffee. They walked to the back of the room and sat in a booth. Immediately, a blond waitress with a diamond stud twinkling on the side of her nose brought them water and menus. "Coffee?"

Toby nodded. "The strongest you have."

"None for me," Eve said.

"I'll be back to take your order in a sec," the waitress said, then turned and walked briskly away.

He looked at Eve. "Sure you don't want anything?"

132

"I'm sure. I'm not hungry." She toyed with the plastic corner of her menu.

He wasn't too hungry either. Maybe it was a bad idea for him to bring her here. Maybe he shouldn't have chased after her when she left.

Then he looked at her blue eyes. Even in their somber state they were pretty, and he knew they were absolutely gorgeous when they shined with happiness. He wished he could put the sparkle back in her eye now. Yet he wasn't sure how.

Tell her. Ever since he'd come back to Youngsville he'd told her he had changed. Now was the time to tell her why.

He couldn't run from the past either.

Eve watched as Toby drank from the steaming cup of coffee. Normally she loved the aroma of fresh brewed java, but now the scent made her stomach turn. She shouldn't have agreed to meet him here. But he was like a magnet, and she was unable to resist his pull. She always had been.

He set the brown mug down. "Remember I told you I know what it's like to lose someone you care about?"

She nodded.

"It happened in Israel," he said.

Over the years she'd seen the reports and video coming out of the Middle East. Some of them had horrified her with their graphic nature, and she knew a lot of the more violent footage had been edited out before it had reached her. *What he must have gone through over there.* Suddenly her problems seemed miniscule in comparison.

"I'd lived there for two years. The first year was exciting—a new experience, a chance to prove myself as an international cameraman. I became really good friends with one reporter over there while we were in Jerusalem. Dave worked for ITV, but we would hang out together during our downtime. Our favorite haunt was this little café on the corner in the marketplace, a few blocks from where I was staying.

"One afternoon we had planned to meet there, but I was running late. When I neared the café, I could see Dave sitting at one of the outside tables, having a drink. I called out his name, and he turned and waved at me."

Toby stopped there, and his face paled. Eve could see how difficult this was for him. Suddenly everything that had occurred earlier that night faded from her mind, and all she could concentrate on was him. On impulse she reached out and took his hand. He entwined his fingers with hers.

"I called out Dave's name," Toby repeated, a little more shakily now. "And he turned and waved. The next second a bus parked in front of the café blew up. It was the last time I ever saw him.

"There was so much death, Eve. Men,

women . . . the children were the hardest to see."
His eyes took on a glazed look. "I never saw
Dave's body. After that explosion, I'm not sure
there was anything left of him."

"Oh, Toby."

"At first I tried not to let it affect me. I mean,
journalists do die in a war zone. It's a fact of the
business. But I had never actually witnessed something like that before. I thought I could handle it,
but after a while, it became impossible."

The waitress came with Toby's order. She
placed a stack of buttermilk pancakes and bacon
in front of him. When she left, he nudged the plate
to the side. A ghost of a smile sat on his lips. "I've
lost my appetite. I'll get a takeout box for this.
Unless you want some of it?"

Even if she was hungry, she couldn't eat. Not
now, not seeing Toby like this. His distress was
palpable. If it was this hard for him to speak of the
memories, she could only guess at the horror he'd
actually gone through.

Their eyes met, and something ignited inside
her. But it was something deeper than the flare of
physical attraction she'd felt for him before.
Something that reached so far inside her soul it
left her breathless. She had a feeling that their
relationship was about to be irrevocably changed.
For better or for worse—she didn't know. She
continued to look at him, affected by the vulnera-

bility in his eyes. It was a quality she'd never seen in him before, and it touched her. Whatever he had to say, she'd stay and listen to him.

Toby wasn't sure he should go on. He wasn't sure he *could* go on. Yet he had a desperate need to tell her everything. He hadn't spoken to anyone about his experiences in Israel since he'd returned to America, not even to his parents. But once he started talking about it, he knew he had to finish.

She ran her thumb across the inside curve of his thumb and finger. The movement was feather-light, almost undetectable.

"After that I just couldn't handle things. I had seen so much death . . . so much useless, pointless death. I started drinking, and hating everything and everybody. Including myself. That's when I decided to leave. So I walked away—a prime job, great money, possibility for more awards—and came back to the United States."

"Was it worth it?"

He smiled wryly. "At the time my co-workers thought the alcohol had fried my brain. And they had a good reason to think that, I pretty much had a bottle in my hand twenty-four-seven, and I was a full-blown drunk at that point. But I don't have any regrets. I don't know what the future holds, either, but I know I made the right decision."

"Why are you telling me all of this?"

"I don't know. Wait . . . yes I do. I'm telling you this because that's what friends do. They share with each other. They help each other get through things."

"Who helped you get over your friend's death?"

He let out a bitter laugh. "Who said I was over it?"

Tears glistened in her eyes. She had wanted him to suffer—and he had. He'd seen his friend die. He'd become an alcoholic. He'd left everything he'd worked so hard for behind. Just thinking about what he had been through made her feel petty—and more than a little guilty.

His gaze went to hers. "There's also another reason I wanted to talk about this. Before I went to Israel, everything was always about me. Whenever I made a decision it was on the basis of how it would affect me, myself and I. No one else existed outside of my personal universe."

"And now?"

"Now I know better. I grew up. I got into AA. I stayed with my parents for a little while in Florida, and did some volunteer work. I learned helping others was much more satisfying than thinking only about myself. I've seen both the depravity of human nature and the generosity of it, and I'd rather be one of the good guys. I haven't always been, but now I'm trying to be."

A dam suddenly broke inside her, and she

fought back her emotions. He had changed. He had been through hell, and came out of it a better person. She could see it in his expression. She could hear it in the tone of his voice. He wasn't just saying these things because he thought she wanted to hear them.

He truly was one of the good guys now.

Chapter Sixteen

"**A**re you going to stand there, or are we going to play?"

Toby glanced down at the basketball he'd been holding in his hands for the past few seconds. He looked across the black asphalt court at Cam, who stood underneath the hoop with his fists on his hips.

"Play," Toby said, at the same time dribbling the ball to the basket and performing a perfect layup. Cam caught the rebound.

"Yeah, real fair, Myers," Cam said, bouncing the ball to half court. "Stand there and act all spaced out, then catch me off guard." He wiped the sweat off his forehead. "I'm not stupid enough to fall for that trick again." With equally smooth moves,

Cam maneuvered around the court, shooting a flawless jump shot over Toby's head. "Ten-ten," he said with a grin. "All tied up. Maybe we missed our calling. Forget being a cameraman and a lawyer. We should have tried out for the NBA." He passed the ball to Toby.

The ball made a resounding thump in his hands when he caught it. "Only one problem," Toby said, attempting to spin the ball on one finger.

"What's that?"

The ball slipped off and bounced to the ground. "We're not very good."

Cam chuckled. "Sure we are. We're superstars—in our own minds at least."

They played for the next thirty minutes, and Toby forced himself to focus on the game. He'd called Cam that morning and suggested meeting at the park for a game of hoops, not wanting to spend all day Saturday moping around his apartment thinking about Eve. He'd taken a chance that his friend would be free, and he was, at least for a while.

"Any big plans for tonight?" Cam said as they took a water break.

Toby wiped the beads of sweat off his face with the back of his hand and tried to sound indifferent. "Nope. Just hanging out with Jerry."

"Now that sounds exciting," Cam said dryly. "Spending an evening watching a kitten chase a ball of string. Almost makes me want to cancel my date with Jen."

"Who's Jen?"

"Only the most delectable woman I've seen in a long time. I met her at the auction, if you can believe it. Sorry, but she even outshines your Eve Norwood."

Toby doubted that. "She's not my Eve," he muttered. *But I wish she was.*

Cam put his bottled water down on the wooden bench. "Sure she isn't. And the hair club for men hasn't been knocking at my door." He pushed back a few strands of blond hair from his receding hairline. "It pains me to say it, but I may have to start investigating some of those options pretty soon."

Picking the basketball off the ground, Toby palmed it with one hand. "Ready to go again?"

"Nope," Cam said, shaking his head. "I'm getting too old for this kind of thing."

"You're only twenty-eight."

"Thirty's just right around the corner. I'm balding, out of shape . . . I better stop before I depress myself." He grinned and grabbed his designer gym bag off the bench. "So when's the big date with Eve?"

"This Friday. And it's not a date." He thought about their talk last night. She hadn't said much after he'd told her about his time in Israel, and they parted ways shortly afterward. Maybe he'd revealed too much too soon. Telling Eve he was an alcoholic over pancakes on a Friday night wasn't the smoothest move he'd ever made. Maybe—

"Toby. Hey slick, you're doing it again." Cam waved his hand in front of Toby's eyes. "What's got you taking these trips out to Lala Land? No, let me guess. Her name starts with the letter E. I bet it ends with an E, and I'm sure there's a V stuck in the middle too."

"Congratulations. You can spell."

"I can do a lot of things," Cam said as he walked away. "Like beating your sorry behind on the basketball court."

"But I won," Toby pointed out.

"That's because I let you." Cam waved his hand and kept on walking. "You won't be so lucky next time," he said, then headed toward the parking lot, unlocking his silver BMW with an automatic remote. "Same time next week?"

"You bet."

After Cam left, Toby shot a few more baskets. The sun had disappeared behind a blanket of gray, billowing clouds. It wasn't long before he discovered playing basketball by himself wasn't the cure for getting Eve out of his mind. He'd have to be dead not to be affected by a woman as beautiful as Eve.

But it was more than her physical looks that

drew him to her. She was the whole package—brains, beauty, and deep inside, a benevolent heart. She'd shown that by her treatment of Shauna after the apartment building burned down, and by her willingness to be auctioned off for charity. He had been fighting his attraction to her from the moment they'd reunited during their first assignment.

He stopped dribbling the ball and glanced around. The park was practically deserted, except for a couple of runners occasionally jogging by. A long, mind-numbing run might do him some good. He went to pick up his keys off the bench when his cell phone rang.

"Hello?"

"Toby?"

"Eve?"

"I hope you don't mind that I called you on your cell. I tried calling you at home but all I got was your answering machine and I couldn't find your pager number, so all I had was the cell phone."

She was rambling. "It's okay, Eve. I don't mind."

"Did I interrupt anything?"

"No. I'm just shooting hoops at the park."

"Good. I didn't want to bother you or anything—"

"You're never a bother."

She paused. "Can I meet you someplace?"

"Sure." He gripped his keys in his hand. She wasn't the only one who was nervous.

"I'll be over in a few minutes. We need to talk."

He hung up the phone, his curiosity at an all-time high. What did she have to say to him that couldn't be said over the phone? He shot some more baskets until she arrived, but missed them all.

She whipped her little compact car into the parking space and got out of it. She was dressed in a pair of khaki shorts and a light blue T-shirt, the outfit enhancing her gorgeous figure.

His stomach tightened at the sight of her. He couldn't read her expression at all as she walked up to him.

Then he saw the glistening tears in her eyes.

"Eve? What's wrong?"

Chapter Seventeen

Toby hated when women cried, having been on the receiving end of more than a couple of manipulating female crying jags. But there was no doubt that Eve's tears were genuine. She'd always kept her tough façade firmly in place. He went to her, resisting the urge to draw her in his arms. Believing he was the source of her sorrow, he asked, "What have I done now?"

"Nothing," she said with a sniff. "I don't even know why I'm crying. The tears suddenly started." She ran the back of her hand over one damp cheek. "I just know I had to see you. And to thank you."

"For what?"

"For talking with me."

"I probably told you too much." He looked away.

"Toby, I'm glad you told me. It made me understand you better. It also made me realize how selfish I've been. All this time you've been so . . . *nice* . . . even though I've been a total witch to you."

"I never blamed you for it."

"I know. It would have been a whole lot easier to stay mad at you if you had." She sniffed. "What's wrong with me, Toby? I used to think I was in such control of my life. I knew what I wanted, when I wanted it, and how I was going to make everything happen. Then my mother died, and then you show up . . . now I feel like I'm on some kind of twisted merry-go-round and I can't get off."

"Eve," he said, moving closer to her. "Life is not about control. It's about living . . . one step at a time. If I learned anything from what happened to Dave, I learned that."

"Well, for a control freak like me, it's easier said than done."

"You don't give yourself enough credit, then."

Suddenly, he felt a fat droplet of water land on his arm. He looked at Eve, and saw three dark, wet circles the size of pennies dampening her light blue shirt. Before he could suggest they seek shelter, the sky opened up completely, sending rain down in watery sheets.

She dug into her purse and pulled out her keys,

opening the door as he ran around to the passenger side of her car. She leaned over and unlocked the door and he jumped in, slamming it against the downpour.

"I guess we're not going anywhere for a while," he said, turning to her. "Not until this rain lets up anyway." He ran his hand through his wet hair.

She dragged the tip of her ring finger underneath her eye, coming away with a smear of black on her finger. She frowned. "I must look like a raccoon," she said, reaching for her purse again. She started digging and retrieved her green compact and a small pack of tissues. "I'm kind of glad we're stuck here for a minute," she said, gesturing to her face. "It's going to take some time to repair the damage."

"I don't know. I think the raccoon look is kind of flattering."

The look she shot him would have been scathing, except for the twist of a smile on her lips. "At least I don't have water dripping from my beard."

With his hand he wiped the moisture from his chin, and then ran his palm against his thigh. He marveled at how easily they had slipped into friendly conversation. It was a relief not to have to measure every word he said to her. "I'm just grateful *you* don't have a beard," he teased.

"Me too," she said with a grin.

The rain tapped a heavy tattoo on the roof of the

vehicle while Eve continued to wipe away the black streaks on her cheeks. "Have you ever thought about shaving it off?"

He brought his hand to his chin and rubbed his fingers over the mat of hair, suddenly self-conscious. "Why? You don't like it?"

She put down her compact and studied him. "It's okay. It just takes some getting used to."

"What's wrong with it?" He angled the rearview mirror so he could see his face. "I keep it trimmed, and it's not like there's food stuck on my chin or anything."

"A little defensive, aren't we?" She snapped her compact shut and returned it to her purse, then leaned back against the headrest, suddenly serious. She let out a long sigh. "My mom died of pancreatic cancer."

"Eve, you don't have to say anything—"

"Yes I do. I just have this need to talk about it. Do you mind?"

He shook his head, remaining silent. He knew exactly how she felt.

"She had only two months from the time she was diagnosed until . . . until she passed away." Eve stared straight ahead. "I was *so* angry, Toby. She was too young to die. And I couldn't do anything to stop it."

"You're not God, Eve."

"I know. But why didn't *he* do anything? I'd

spent so many years in school, interning, then working on my career. When you left I threw myself even deeper into my work, isolating my life from everyone but my mom. Then she was gone, and I was so incredibly lonely. Still, I thought I could handle it. Handle her death, handle the job, handle the emptiness." She turned and looked at him. "I've turned into this person I don't know anymore. I realize now that I can't handle anything."

He shifted in the seat. "Yes you can, Eve. So what if you take a detour now and then? Everyone needs some slack, even the great Eve Norwood."

She laughed. "I'm not so great. Well, maybe a little bit great."

He smiled in return. "Just a little."

The rain suddenly eased up, and beams of sunlight shone in the storm's wake. Droplets of water rolled slowly down the windshield.

"I guess I should be going," she said after a long period of silence. She looked at him again. "Thanks for listening to me."

"Anytime." He opened the door. Their relationship had definitely turned a corner. He wanted to stay, to talk to her some more. But he wasn't about to push her. "See you Friday night?"

"Yes." She glanced at him. "I never thought I would say this, but I'm actually looking forward to it."

Me too, he thought to himself. *Me too.*

Chapter Eighteen

Eve scrutinized her image in the dressing room's full-length mirror and tried to ignore the tightness in her stomach. In a few short hours she and Toby would be on their way to Cleveland for their date on the *Nautica Queen*. After inspecting her wardrobe that morning, she decided at the last minute to go shopping for a new dress, and ended up at The Perfect Fit, an upscale boutique in downtown Youngsville.

"It's not a date," she whispered to her reflection. She'd uttered the reminder for what seemed like the thousandth time that week. Of course it didn't keep her heart from slamming against her ribcage each time she thought about tonight.

She stepped out of the dressing room and went

to look at her reflection in the boutique's three-way mirror. She didn't particularly like what she saw.

"It looks splendid on you," the trim, copper-haired saleslady said as she came up behind her. The lines in her face betrayed her age. Eve surmised the woman was at least in her sixties, but her figure and style of dress made her look years younger.

Eve untwisted the nearly invisible spaghetti strap and adjusted it over her right shoulder. "I don't know," she said, eyeing the thin sheath of material. Two layers of scarlet silk flowed over her torso and hips until the hem barely skimmed her knees. "It seems a bit . . . revealing."

"Well, it's not as if you don't have the figure for it," the saleswoman pointed out. "And flesh is very 'in' right now. You can never leave too little to a man's imagination."

Eve frowned. 'Tempestuous siren' was definitely *not* the image she wanted to portray tonight. "Do you have anything a little more sophisticated?"

The woman peered at Eve over her tortoise shell reading glasses. "Not too many women can wear a dress like that."

"Neither can I."

"Very well." She removed her glasses and let them dangle around her neck from a glittering rhinestone chain. "I'll see what else we have in your size."

Several moments later the saleswoman returned with a light purple dress draped on a hanger. "I believe this one is more suited to what you had in mind."

She entered the dressing room, took off the red dress and slipped on the lavender one. It had short, capped sleeves and the scoop neckline wasn't cut too low. The fabric was soft panne velvet, and the hemline reached mid-calf.

"How does the dress fit, Ms. Norwood?"

"Okay, I guess." With a critical eye she stared at her reflection again, automatically sucking in her tummy.

"Why don't you come out and use the three-way mirror?" the saleswoman suggested. "You'll get a better idea of how it looks on you."

Seeing herself in triplicate didn't help her make a decision. "I'm not sure about the purple."

"Not *purple* . . . this hue is called hyacinth. And here's the final touch." She draped a long, narrow piece of matching silk around Eve's shoulders. "Pashmina," she cooed.

"I always thought they were called shawls." Eve let the soft fabric drop into the crooks of her arms.

"Pashmina silk, dear. It's what the garment is made of."

"Oh." Eve looked in the mirror again. She had to admit the dress fit well, accentuating all her good features and diminishing the ones that weren't so great. The fabric felt wonderful against her skin, and she had an amethyst necklace in her jewelry box that would go perfectly with the dress. "A *hyacinth* necklace," she whispered.

"Pardon?"

Eve shook her head. "Never mind." She glanced at the price tag dangling from the dress and winced. The boutique was renowned for its fabulous selections—and hefty prices.

"Is this for a special occasion?"

"No . . . well, sort of." Eve gave a brief explanation of why she needed the dress.

"I see," the woman said, then smiled. "Hyacinth is definitely your color. I'm sure your young man will adore you in this dress."

"I don't know about that." She frowned at the small glimmer of hope she felt that Toby might like the outfit. "I'll take it," she said quickly, before she changed her mind.

The saleswoman's heavily painted eyes lit up in delight. "Wonderful! You've made an excellent choice." She reached for the shawl. "I'll just take this up front while you change. Now, have you thought about shoes? We have a pair of silver Manolo Blahniks that would look simply divine on you."

Eve almost asked to see them, but she shook her head. She'd spent enough already. "Actually, I have a pair at home that will work."

Later that afternoon in her apartment, a couple of hours before Toby was to arrive, Eve hung the dress on the back of her closet door. She stared at it for a moment, and the butterflies she'd kept at bay for most of the day now fluttered wildly in her stomach. There was no denying it—she was nervous. Despite her attempts to convince herself otherwise, she felt as if she was going on her first date. Even the hot cup of raspberry tea she'd prepared didn't have its normal soothing effects.

She and Toby had worked only one assignment in the past week—a man who won $12 million in the Ohio lottery donated all of his money to the local library system for upgrades and new programs. But they had also called each other every day after work, talking for hours. In fact, they had talked more in the past couple of days than in all the months they had dated. They shared everything— their hopes, dreams, fears—everything but their actual feelings. Or at least her feelings about him, which seemed to be changing by the minute.

Still jittery, she went into the bathroom and started applying her makeup. *Calm down! This is not important . . . it's work related . . . we're just friends . . . nothing more.* However, the repetitive thoughts did little to change her feelings.

Slipping her feet into a pair of strappy, silver-heeled sandals, she reached for her shawl when she heard the doorbell chime. *He's here.*

Opening the door, her breath caught. She'd never seen him look so incredible. The suit was midnight blue, the cut of the jacket emphasizing his broad shoulders and tapered waist. His silk tie was a lighter shade of blue, a nice contrast to his crisp white shirt. Almost as an afterthought, she inhaled the scent of his cologne, and hid her smile. He was wearing the fresh, woodsy fragrance she particularly liked.

"Hi," he said.

"Hi," she replied softly, the only word she could coherently speak.

His gaze traveled her body from head to toe. "You look . . ."

He paused, and she could feel her face heating up. *Does he hate hyacinth? Is there something in my teeth? Why is he just standing there, not saying anything?*

"Beautiful," he finally said with a smile. "You look beautiful, Eve."

She exhaled with relief, warmed to her toes by his compliment. "You do too. Wait. I don't mean you look beautiful—"

He laughed. "I know what you mean."

They stood there for a few moments, not saying anything. Then she remembered herself. "Do you want to come in?" she asked, holding the door open a little bit more.

"Sure." He stepped sideways into the apartment, keeping his hands behind his back. She shut the door. Not knowing what else to say, Eve stared down at her feet.

"Nice shoes," he said, following her gaze. "Oh, this is for you." With one hand he offered her a paper bag. The top had been folded over several times.

She lifted a brow. "What is this?" she said, taking the bag from him. Curious, she unfolded it and peered in. With a gasp of surprise, she reached inside and withdrew two navy-blue shoes, the ones she'd left in one of the WCBH vans a couple of weeks ago. "I went back to look for these the day after the Brewster story," she said, turning the pair of dress pumps over in her hand. "They weren't there. I'd just assumed another crew had thrown them away, considering what one of them was covered with."

A slightly sheepish expression crossed his face. "I cleaned them up a little for you."

"A little?" she said in astonishment as she inspected each shoe. There wasn't a trace of dirt, straw, or manure anywhere on the soles, and the leather had been polished until it gleamed. They looked almost brand new. "Thank you." She put the shoes back in the bag and set it down on the floor.

"This is for you too," he said, bringing his other hand from behind his back. He extended a single red rose to her. "I know this isn't an actual date, but I didn't think you'd mind a flower from a friend."

No, she didn't mind. She took the rose from him. Unable to resist, she touched a silken petal, then brought the flower up to her nose, hiding her smile behind the delicate bud.

"Ready to go?" he asked, opening the door for her.

She picked up her scarf that was draped over the beige recliner. "Yes," she said, giving him a genuine smile. "I'm more than ready."

The two-hour drive to Cleveland passed quickly. She and Toby conversed the entire time. She could easily see Toby as a good friend. Even a best friend.

If only she could stop herself from wishing for more.

They turned into the parking lot at the *Nautica Queen* dock. Toby exited his truck and walked around to the other side. He opened the door and held out his hand to Eve, then helped her out of the vehicle.

"Keeping up appearances?" she joked, despite being flattered by his special attention. She noticed the small crowd of people walking toward the ship.

"Should we?" he asked, closing the door.

He was still holding her hand. The warmth of his palm against hers felt good. No, not just good. It felt *incredible*. And so, so very right.

"Maybe we should," she murmured. Feeling the tiniest bit devious for taking advantage of the situation, she entwined her fingers in his. "After all, you never know who might be watching."

He grinned, and clasped her hand more tightly. "That's right. You never know."

They started walking toward the docks when Eve thought of something. She turned to Toby. "Where's your ENG equipment?"

"Um," he said, suddenly looking sheepish. "I forgot it."

"You did?"

"Guess I had my mind on something else."

"So how are we going to report on this cruise?"

"We'll just have to wing it." He grinned and squeezed her hand. "Come on, we have a boat to catch."

He didn't seem too worried about blowing the story. For some reason and for the first time ever in her career, she wasn't either. They'd explain it to Brianne, somehow. Following his lead, they headed for the docks.

Moments later, they boarded the ship, and entered the main dining area.

"Ah, Ms. Norwood!"

"I recognize that voice," Toby muttered.

They turned around and saw Eloise Ruiz, resplendent in a glittery, silver-sequined ensemble. She looked bright enough to light up a small town. A smile twitched on her lips. "It looks like you two are doing fine, so I'll be on my way." Giving them a knowing look, she dashed off, greeting the other auction participants and their dates.

Soon they left the dock and started their cruise on Lake Erie. For the first thirty minutes, Eve and Toby mixed and mingled with the other bachelors and bachelorettes. Brilliant flashes of light sparked in the room as the photographer Eloise had hired snapped numerous photos of the guests. In the corner Eve spied Alfred Minnefield with his statuesque date. She returned his cheerful wave.

"How about we get some fresh air," Toby suggested.

"Sounds good."

They left, and entered the outside deck. It was fairly deserted. They walked over to the edge of the ship, a cool blast of air greeting them. Eve shivered, and wrapped her shawl more securely around her shoulders. But it did little to keep her warm.

"Are you cold?"

She nodded. "I should have brought a sweater or something."

He slid closer to her until there was only a fraction of space between them. "Here, you can borrow my jacket," he said, slipping it off and wrapping it securely around her shoulders.

Involuntarily, she tugged the lapels closer to her and breathed in deeply, inhaling the lingering scent of cologne. The warmth of the jacket immediately soaked into her.

"Better?"

Oh, yes. Most definitely. "Won't you be cold?"

"I'm fine."

They stood there for a few moments, side by side, leaning against the rail. Eve looked down into the churning, dark water.

Toby leaned over and spoke softly near her ear. "What are you thinking about?"

"Nothing really," she replied, her gaze still fixed on the water below. "Just how much I'm enjoying this evening."

"I am too."

"You are?" His admission surprised her.

"Of course I am. Why wouldn't I?"

She turned and faced him. "It's not like we're here under normal circumstances. And I wasn't sure we'd be able to pull off the whole 'pretending we're on a date thing.' " Tugging his jacket closer, she gave him a crooked smile. "We seem to have fooled everyone, though."

"Including ourselves?"

She stilled. What did he mean by that?

He looked straight ahead at the towering buildings on the shore, and she was struck by his handsome profile. Something stirred deep within her, an emotion so intense it made her knees weak.

A sudden realization stole over her. She was tired of fighting her feelings, of battling her attraction to Toby. She'd spent the last month trying to convince herself that there was nothing between them, that the sparks they'd created when they were together had died long ago. But she didn't believe that, not anymore. There was plenty of fire between them. If she couldn't admit that to him, she could at least admit it to herself.

"There's something I need to talk to you about," he said, immediately jerking her out of her thoughts. Knowing her emotions were dangerously close to the surface, she tucked them inside her heart, struggling to keep her expression impassive.

He spoke again. "It's been weighing on my mind for a while. I figure now is as good a time as any to bring it up." He looked at her, his expression solemn.

Her stomach dropped.

"I can't keep living a lie," he continued, turning to face her.

A dozen thoughts ran through her head. *He's ending our friendship . . . he's secretly engaged . . . he took a job at another station . . .*

"I have to be completely honest. I ran from the truth before. I won't do it again."

He was absolutely serious. Her anxiety heightened a notch.

"Eve . . ." he whispered, her name dying on his lips. He brushed the back of his knuckles against her face, and then tenderly swept a strand of her windblown hair behind her ear. When his hand curved around her cheek, skimming across her skin in a slow, tantalizing movement, she was completely undone.

Toby's heart slammed in his chest as he withdrew his hand. He was taking a chance, and he knew it. He was risking it all—their friendship, and more than likely, their professional relationship. But he didn't care. Nothing mattered right now except telling Eve the truth.

Since their talk she'd appeared more relaxed than he had ever seen her. He also noticed how she smiled and laughed more readily, and was no longer on the defensive with him. Seeing the softer side of Eve made him like her even more. More than a coworker. And much, much more than a friend.

Whether she felt the same about him, he didn't know. And if she didn't, he would find a way to accept it. However, he couldn't keep his feelings secret anymore. He didn't want to.

"Toby—"

"Shhh," he said, placing his finger on her lips.

Her eyes widened with surprise, and he half expected her to jerk away from him. He wouldn't blame her. He hadn't expected to touch her like this. But now that he had, he didn't want to let go.

"I need to say this to you," he continued. "*Without* interruptions." Reluctantly he pulled away, and shoved his hands into his pockets. "Eve, this friendship thing between us . . . I'm afraid it's not working out."

"I knew it," she whispered. Turning her back to him, she fought against the pain in her heart. His teasing touch a moment ago was just that—a tease. Something to butter her up with, to prepare her for the big letdown. "I knew you were going to end this."

"End what?" He went to her, laying his hands on her shoulders. "Eve, I don't want to end—"

She whirled around, her eyes stinging with unshed tears. He'd aimed the knife at her heart, and in her usual self-destructive way, she would drive it home. "You want honesty? Well here's some truth for you. I did it again, Toby. Can you believe it? I let you get to me. How stupid and naïve is that? I've fallen for you all over again, and now you're going to dump me. Although I guess you can't do that because we're not even dating." A wave of heartache washed through her. "At least you're telling me to my face this time."

His mouth dropped open, his features frozen in shock. "What did you just say?"

She huffed, and blinked back her tears. *Why not make my humiliation complete?* "At least you're telling me—"

"No, before that."

She had to stop and think for a moment. What did she say? The words had flowed out of her in such a blind rush she couldn't recall them right away.

He moved closer to her, and cradled her face in his hands. "The part about how you've fallen for me?"

Eve's toes curled in her sandals. "Oh . . . that part." His expression didn't jibe with someone about to walk away from a friendship. In fact, the desire she saw in his eyes revealed the exact opposite.

He caressed her cheek with his hand. "I think this is the part where I tell you how I fell for this reporter . . ."

Her heart stopped beating.

"Who is talented beyond description, and beautiful beyond words."

She stopped breathing.

"Perhaps insanity is her *only* flaw, because for some crazy reason, she just said she liked me too." He lowered his head and captured her mouth in a gentle, yet searing kiss, one that reached down into the depths of her soul. "I've been dying to do that all night," he said huskily.

"Ah," she mumbled, incapable of saying a rational sentence. She glanced around the deck of the boat, glad that they were still alone. She licked her lips self-consciously, noting that they were still warm from his kiss. She tried speaking again. "So you're saying we're not friends?"

He laughed. "After that kiss, I hope not."

She smiled, and pressed her cheek against his chest. His heart thumped rapidly in her ear. Reveling in the feel of his strong arms around her, she lifted her head and looked up at him. The hair on his chin brushed against her forehead, tickling her skin. Yes, she could easily get used to his beard.

"I do have more than one flaw, you know," she said with a teasing grin.

He kissed her again, much longer this time. When their lips parted, it was all she could do to remain standing. *Wow.*

"You may have a few flaws, Eve Norwood," he whispered in her ear. "But kissing definitely isn't one of them."

Chapter Nineteen

"**I** don't think he likes it," Eve said, frowning.

Toby came up behind her. "Give him some time," he said. "He's just investigating it right now. Once he figures out what it's for, he'll use it."

"Yeah, just like he uses his bed, right?"

"Can I help it if he prefers to sleep with me?"

They both continued watching Jerry as he checked out Eve's latest present—a deluxe scratching post. Since meeting Jerry four months ago, right before their first 'official' date, Eve had been smitten with the cat.

Gracefully rising on his hind legs, Jerry extended a paw and cautiously batted one of the tails of the bright red bow she had placed on top of the scratching post.

"Come here," she said, stepping forward and scooping the cat up in her arms. Jerry instantly settled against her, closing his eyes as she scratched beneath his chin.

"You're spoiling him," Toby said, feeling inexplicably jealous of the attention his cat was receiving from Eve.

"Who else am I going to spoil?" She moved closer to him until Jerry was the only thing that separated them.

The heady scent of her perfume filled his nostrils. "I know someone who wouldn't mind a little TLC," he murmured, taking Jerry out of her arms.

"I can't imagine who that would be."

He let Jerry fall lightly to the floor and drew her into his embrace. "You get three guesses." He nuzzled her neck. "But the first two don't count."

She giggled against his mouth as he planted a light kiss on her lips. "You know, I'm not sure if I can get used to you without a beard."

With a groan he pulled away. "I thought you didn't like it," he said, exasperated. Shaving it off had been more of an ordeal than he'd thought.

She ran her fingers across his now-smooth cheek. "I didn't . . . but now I'm not so sure. You look really different now."

"Different in a good way or a bad way?"

"Never in a bad way," she said, touching his cheek again.

The timer on the oven started beeping. "I better go get that," He took her hand and pressed a kiss to her palm.

Eve sniffed as Toby went into the kitchen. "Smells wonderful. What have you made to-night?" she asked as she sat down at the card table in the tiny dining area in his apartment. "Something Mexican?"

"Bingo." He pulled out an enchilada casserole, then brought it out and placed it on a stoneware trivet in the middle of the table. Eve had put out the place settings earlier, including two long tapered candles. Cooking dinner for her on Sunday nights had become a ritual for them, ever since her first attempt at preparing him a meal had gone down in flames—literally.

His cooking wasn't all that much better, but at least he lived closer to the fire department.

As soon as Toby sat down, Eve's cell phone rang. "Ignore it," he said, scooping out a healthy serving of the casserole. "You're way too attached to that thing anyway."

"But what if it's important?" She retrieved her phone. "Eve Norwood."

"Eve, its Elizabeth. Are you sitting down?"

"Yes," she said, alarm gripping her. "What's wrong?"

"Wrong? Nothing's wrong!"

"But it's Saturday night. You never call me on a Saturday."

"I couldn't wait until Monday. I just got home from a trip to the Poconos—wouldn't you know my cell phone doesn't work in the mountains? Anyway, I just checked my messages and—are you ready for this?" Her agent took a dramatic pause. "The network brass at ABC *loved* your audition tape."

"They did?" Eve asked, stunned.

"They want to interview you ASAP. How soon can you get to New York?"

Excitement raced through her. Immediately, her mind started whirling. "I'll have to call the airline and make reservations—"

"The network will take care of all that," Elizabeth interjected. "You need to be here on Monday."

"Monday? That soon?"

"Sweetheart," Elizabeth said with a chuckle. "Monday isn't soon enough. They wanted you here yesterday."

Yesterday? Eve could barely contain her enthusiasm. "That's wonderful! I'll be there first thing on Monday."

"Perfect! I'll let them know. This is it, Eve. Your big break. You deserve it."

Eve clicked off the phone and slowly laid it down on the table, still in a daze. Her dream was finally coming true, and it was only starting to sink in.

"Eve?"

Her gaze shot to Toby. In her excitement she'd forgotten about him. "That was my agent. The network . . . ABC . . . they want to interview me." A huge smile spread across her face. "I can't believe it. I had almost given up hope of them ever calling me." Suddenly realizing everything she had to do to get ready, she snatched up her cell phone and shot from her seat. "I've got to go. I have to talk to Brianne, then get packed—"

"Hold up a minute," he said, touching her arm. "Shouldn't you give this some more thought?"

She slipped on her wool coat. "What's there to think about? This has been my dream, you know that. I've spent my entire career working for this chance."

He stood up. "But are you sure?"

Her fingers remained immobile on the last button of her coat. She stared at him in disbelief. "I thought you'd be excited for me," she said, her own happiness dimming. "Instead, you sound like you're trying to talk me out of it."

Toby stood up and went to her. "No, not exactly . . ."

Her irritation escalated. She wanted to share her good fortune with him. He should be hugging her, offering to take her to the airport, not sulking like a spoiled child who had one of his favorite toys taken away. Determined not to skirt the issue, she asked him straight out, "Do you have a problem with this, Toby?"

He shoved his hand through his hair and faced her, his expression grave. "Just where do I fit in your dream, Eve? If you get this job, what happens to us?"

"I . . . I don't know. I haven't had a chance to think about it."

The hurt that entered his eyes lanced her heart. "I'm not interested in a long-distance relationship," he said dully.

She grabbed his hands and closed the space between them. "Then come with me. I'm sure you could freelance in New York."

He shook his head, dropping her hands, and taking a step back. "I can't go with you," he said, his voice cracking. "Don't ask me to move back to New York, Eve. I left it behind for good."

"So you expect me to give up everything?" She fought the frustration rising again within her. "Don't you think you're being unfair?"

"What are you giving up?" he asked hotly. "Everything you need is here. A great job. Me." A shadow passed over his features. "Am I not enough for you?"

She didn't know what to say. How could she explain it so he would understand? She searched her mind for the words, but came up empty.

"I see," he said, moving even farther away.

"Toby—"

He held up his hand. "Your career is important to you. I knew that going in. I just never thought it would be more important than me." He crammed his hands into the pockets of his coat. "Go ahead and do what you have to do."

"Toby, wait—"

Ignoring her attempts to stop him, he turned around, and left the room.

And left her heart in pieces.

Chapter Twenty

Eve sank back in the back seat of the black and yellow taxi cab. Glancing at her watch, she saw she had plenty of time to get to the airport and catch her 6 A.M. flight. As the cab pulled into the departure area, Eve stared blankly out of the window into the dusky light of early morning, trying to forget about her fight with Toby on Sunday night. Why couldn't he be supportive of her in this? He'd already had his opportunity with the network. What right did he have to deny hers? She should be bursting with hope right now, not wallowing in despair.

Her cell phone rang. She dug it out of her purse. "Hello?"

"Eve, its Elizabeth," she said, excitement evident in her voice. "Just calling to make sure you're on your way."

Eve couldn't help a slight smile. Her agent had enough enthusiasm for the both of them.

"In a few hours you'll be a correspondent with ABC news," she gushed.

Eve leaned forward slightly as the cab shifted into park. "I don't have the job yet," Eve said. "This is just an interview, right?"

"The interview process is a formality. They'll take one look at you and hire you on the spot."

"We'll see."

"You don't sound very confident," Elizabeth remarked. "You sound more like you've lost your best friend."

"I have," Eve whispered to herself.

"What was that?"

"Nothing."

"Whatever is bothering you, put it out of your mind. Now's not the time to lose your focus. You won't get too many chances like this."

So don't blow it. Eve silently finished her agent's pep talk. Elizabeth was right. It had taken Eve so long to pique the interest of the network that she knew this would be her only opportunity. Mentally shoving away her problems with Toby, she grasped the door handle of the car.

"Now as soon as we get to the hotel, we'll check in, and then have breakfast. Right after that we'll

catch a cab to the network and do the interview."
Elizabeth continued to map out their day in detail.
"Do you mind if we have an early supper? I have
another meeting at six tonight, then I have to catch
a plane to the west coast at eleven."

Elizabeth's schedule sounded mind-boggling.
But then her agent was always on the go. "When
do you find time to relax?" Eve asked.

Elizabeth's throaty chuckle filled the phone.
"Relax? Honey, I forgot the meaning of that word
a long time ago. And you might as well forget
about relaxing too, once you get this job. I'll hang
up now, don't want you to miss that plane.
Security is so tight at the airports now. You don't
want to cut it too close in case they stop and check
your shoes or something."

At the airport, Eve surprisingly breezed through
security. When she arrived at the gate, she had
plenty of time before her flight was scheduled to
leave. She put her carry-on suitcase on the floor
and sat down in one of the green plastic leather
seats. She glanced up at the television monitor.
WCBH's morning newscast was on. She turned
away.

"Is anyone sitting here?"

Eve looked up at the young woman standing in
front of her, holding a tiny baby in her arms. She
gestured to the empty seat next to her. "No. Go
right ahead."

"Thanks." She sat down and put her white and red diaper bag on the floor, then adjusted the pink fuzzy blanket wrapped around the child. After a few seconds she began tapping her foot frantically on the floor, causing her leg to twitch. "This is our first flight," she said in a heavy New York accent. She gave Eve an uneasy smile. "I'm a little nervous."

"Are you traveling alone?"

"Yes. We're going to visit my mom—she lives in Queens." She looked down at the baby. "She hasn't seen MacKenzie yet, and since my husband started a new job here, he doesn't have vacation time for a while. I wanted to give my mom the chance to hold her first grandchild while she was still a newborn."

"How old is she?" she asked. "MacKenzie, I mean."

"Two months."

Eve's brow lifted in surprise. "That's really young."

As if she knew she was the topic of conversation, MacKenzie started to cry. Her mother peeled back the blanket, revealing a plump, rosy-cheeked infant, her mouth wide open in full wail.

"I just gave her a bottle. She must want her pacifier." The woman glanced down at the bag. "Would you mind handing it to me? It's in the side pocket."

"Sure," Eve replied, and gave her the pink and

purple pacifier. The young woman popped it in her daughter's mouth, and MacKenzie quieted, her piercing cries replaced by loud sucking noises.

Eve watched as the baby's mother ran a finger-tip across her daughter's plump cheek. The tender scene caused a sudden, unfamiliar longing deep inside her. She didn't consider herself the nurturing type, and she'd never really decided whether she wanted children or not. But at that moment a vision flashed through her mind. Of her holding a baby. *Her* baby. One that had chocolate-brown eyes—just like Toby.

"Ladies and gentlemen, Flight Four-two-seven departing to LaGuardia is ready to board," a nasally voice resounded over the intercom. "Those of you who need special assistance, or are traveling with small children, please come forward for preboarding."

"That's me," the woman said, rising. She picked up her bag. "Have a good flight."

"You too," Eve replied as the woman walked away. While she waited for her turn to board, her mind began to spin, matching the inner turmoil she felt inside. She thought about her job, Toby, even little baby MacKenzie. A few months ago she would have known exactly which path she would take in life—the one that led straight to New York. Yet now that she was on her way there, nothing seemed clearcut anymore.

She stared at the ticket in her hand. Her ticket to the big time. But she was giving up so much. Would it be worth it?

"Yes," she whispered, standing up. Shoving her ticket into her bag, she left the terminal, becoming calmer with each step. She was squandering an opportunity she'd been working so hard for. But suddenly that didn't matter anymore. Everything she needed—and wanted—was here. In Youngsville.

"Miss?" The attendant called out to her. "I just announced the final boarding call."

"I'm not boarding," Eve said.

The young woman frowned. "Are you sure?"

"Absolutely."

She hurried through the airport, wondering if she'd ruined her future with Toby. She'd left him in the blink of an eye, just as he'd done to her years ago. Was he as angry as she had been? Was he hurting as much as she had?

How could she have done that to him?

Halting her steps, she retrieved her cell phone, and punched in his number, her hands shaking. No answer. She dialed his home phone. The machine picked up. Her spirits sank. Was he ignoring her? She wouldn't blame him.

Her purse slipped off her shoulder, falling to the ground. She bent to pick it up, only to see someone else come up behind her and take it.

"Hey!" she shouted, spinning around. "That's my—"

"I thought you might need some help with this."

Toby.

She remained frozen in place, shock preventing her from moving. He held her purse in one hand, a single rose in the other. His leather jacket was unzipped, and she could see a faded T-shirt underneath: I LOVE NY, with a big red heart. He gave her a tentative smile, as if he wasn't sure of what her reaction would be.

She reacted the only way she could.

Wrapping her arms around him, she breathed in the wonderful scents of cologne and leather. "What are you doing here?"

"I came to see you off," he whispered, hugging her more tightly. "Did you miss your flight?"

"Yes," she said, pulling back slightly.

"Well, I'm kind of glad you did. I came here to tell you I'm sorry for not supporting you. And I'll follow you anywhere, whether it's New York City or Timbuktu."

Her heart thrummed in her chest. "You're willing to do that . . . for me?"

He nodded, touching her cheek. "For both of us. I love you, Eve."

Her heart thrummed in her chest. Oh, how she loved this man. Knowing what he was willing to do to help her reach her dream floored her. Lucky for both of them her dreams had changed. "Don't pack your bags anytime soon."

"What?"

"You were right, Toby. I don't need to be in New York to be happy. Everything I need to be happy is right here . . . with you."

His eyes widened. "So you're staying?"

"I'm staying."

Drawing her into his arms, he kissed her, a bone-melting, passion-inducing kiss. When he withdrew, the look in his eyes almost had her swooning on the spot.

"With a little practice, we might actually get this kissing thing down pat," he teased.

She gave him a wicked grin. "You know what they say," she said, drawing his mouth down to hers. "Practice makes perfect."

Chapter Twenty-one

Five months later

"I have to say, Eve, Brianne sure knows how to throw a party." Toby took a sip of cranberry punch. "There must be at least fifty people here."

Eve glanced around the spacious backyard from her seat on the patio of Brianne's elegant colonial. Music filtered through an outdoor stereo system, and the guests were mingling, laughing, and having a good time.

"I'm glad to see Elizabeth made it," he commented.

"Me too." She watched as her agent mixed in with the crowd, obviously working the party. It brought a smile to Eve's lips. It had taken time, but Elizabeth had eventually understood Eve's decision. Although she no longer represented Eve, the two women had remained good friends.

Eve looked around the expansive area again. The air was spiced with the aroma of freshly mown grass, blending with the light scent of roses coming from Brianne's extensive garden. Briefly, she wondered how Brianne afforded such a house on her salary, but Eve sent the thought away. It was really none of her business. Still, it did seem rather mysterious; a young, single woman living in such a large house. *Okay, enough with the reporter's curiosity. I'm here to have fun . . . to celebrate . . . to—*

"What are you thinking about?" Toby asked, interrupting her thoughts.

"Nothing."

"Don't give me that. I can practically hear the wheels turning in your mind."

"If you must know, I was admiring Brianne's house."

Toby glanced around. "It is beautiful," he remarked. "Which reminds me, we should probably start house-hunting soon. I don't want to live the rest of my life in an apartment."

"Me neither."

His eyes twinkled mischievously. "Especially if we plan to fill our home with the pitter patter of little feet."

She feigned ignorance. "You mean Jerry? He doesn't take up much room."

He laughed. "I said feet, not paws."

Shifting closer to her on the wrought iron bench seat, he picked up her left hand. The pear-shaped diamond sparkled in the afternoon sunlight. "Two more weeks," he said, crossing his ankle over his knee, "and you'll be Mrs. Toby Myers. Think you can handle it?"

"Oh, I can handle it, all right," she said dryly. A smile twitched at the corners of her mouth. "The question is, can you?"

"You'll find out on our honeymoon," he whispered, then kissed her cheek. "I love it when you turn red like that."

"Hmmph." She spotted Brianne and Cam talking near the heart-shaped ice sculpture. "They seem to be getting along well," she pointed out.

"Playing matchmaker, are you?"

"I don't know," she said, looking at him. "Should I?"

He grew serious. "I'm not sure. Cam's going through some problems right now."

"He still won't tell you what's wrong?"

Toby shook his head, tracing invisible circles on Eve's hand with his thumb. "I've tried talking to him. He just cracks a joke and blows me off. He says I'm getting too serious in my old age." Rising from the bench, he brought Eve up with him. "I don't want to talk about Cam or Brianne right now," he said in a low voice. "I want you to come with me."

She let him lead her away from the crowd. "Where are we going?"

"You'll see."

"Toby, we can't leave our own engagement party!"

He chuckled. "We're not leaving. We're simply disappearing for a while."

A surge of anticipation flowed through her as she followed him inside the house. They nodded to the small group of people huddled around the kitchen bar, and then continued down the hallway.

"Close your eyes," he said, grabbing her hand. When she didn't immediately comply, he squeezed her fingers. "Just do it, Eve."

"Of all the silly—" She shut her eyes at his quelling look. "Okay, they're closed. Now what?"

She heard a creaking sound before she was dragged unceremoniously into a small, confined space. The door squeaked shut, and even with her lids closed she could tell they were plunged into darkness.

"Why are we in the coat closet?"

"You peeked," he said with mock disappointment.

"I can smell the mothballs."

"Brianne must be the only person in the world who still uses those things."

"At least the only person under eighty years old." She opened her eyes, unable to see anything. "What are we doing here?"

He ran his hand up and down her arm. "Can you think of any other place more private than this?"

"I can think of a thousand places more *comfortable* than this," she stated sharply. "I'm not sure our boss would appreciate us being in here."

"Trust me. She won't mind a bit."

"Can we at least have some light?"

He turned it on. "Feel better now?"

"Much. Now, explain to me again why we're here?"

"I wanted to give you this." He reached up on the top shelf of the closet and pulled down a small, narrow rectangular box.

She eyed it suspiciously. "Is this for me?"

"Yes." He handed the box to her. "An early wedding gift."

"Now I feel guilty," she said, fingering the red bow. "I didn't get you anything."

"Don't worry about it." He looked at her eagerly. "Aren't you going to open it?"

Gingerly she loosened the bow, and then lifted the lid. "Oh, Toby," she said, taking the desk nameplate out of the box. The gold metal shone in the dim light of the closet. *Eve Norwood-Myers.* "I love it. Thank you," she said softly.

He stepped toward her. "Is that the best you can do?" he said, a playful spark in his eye.

She was up to the challenge. She rested her hand on his clean-shaven cheek, then trailed a finger over his new goatee, which she absolutely loved. He had definitely learned the fine art of compromise.

"I assure you I can do much, *much* better." Stepping into his arms, she kissed him. "How was that?"

"Hmm," he said, a smile slowly spreading across his face. "Pretty good."

"Pretty good?" she said, lifting a brow.

"Yep." His grin grew even wider.

"I'll show you pretty good." She drew him closer, then kissed him until neither one of them could breathe. "Better?"

"Oh yeah," he said, whispering in her ear. "But now you've raised the bar, Mrs. Soon-to-be Eve Norwood-Myers. I'll expect to be kissed like that for the rest of my life."

Eve hugged him tightly. "Oh, you will be, Toby Myers. I guarantee you will be."